ETERNITY NOW: VOLUME 4

DEATH TO LIFE

PAUL

NET

THOMAS NELSON
Since 1798

www.ThomasNelson.com

NET NT Series Eternity Now: *Volume 4: Death to Life*

Copyright © 2022 by Thomas Nelson, a division of HarperCollins Christian Publishing, Inc.

Published in Nashville, Tennessee, by Thomas Nelson. Thomas Nelson is a registered trademark of HarperCollins Christian Publishing, Inc.

The NET Bible, New English Translation
Copyright © 1996, 2019 by Biblical Studies Press, LLC

NET Bible® is a registered trademark.

For free access to the NET Bible, the complete set of 60,000 translators' notes, and Bible study resources, visit:

    bible.org
    netbible.org
    netbible.com

Used by permission. All rights reserved.

Library of Congress Control Number: 2021952038

This Bible was set in the Thomas Nelson NET Typeface, created at the 2K/DENMARK A/S type foundry.

All rights reserved.

Printed in the United States of America

22 23 24 25 25 27 28 29 30 / TRM / 10 9 8 7 6 5 4 3 2 1

CONTENTS

TO THE READER

AN INTRODUCTION TO THE NEW ENGLISH TRANSLATION

You have been born anew ... through the living and enduring word of God.
1 Peter 1:23

The New English Translation (NET) is the newest complete translation of the original biblical languages into English. In 1995 a multidenominational team of more than twenty-five of the world's foremost biblical scholars gathered around the shared vision of creating an English Bible translation that could overcome old challenges and boldly open the door for new possibilities. The translators completed the first edition in 2001 and incorporated revisions based on scholarly and user feedback in 2003 and 2005. In 2019 a major update reached its final stages. The NET's unique translation process has yielded a beautiful, faithful English Bible for the worldwide church today.

What sets the NET Bible apart from other translations? We encourage you to read the full story of the NET's development and additional details about its translation philosophy at netbible.com/net-bible-preface. But we would like to draw your attention to a few features that commend the NET to all readers of the Word.

TRANSPARENT AND ACCOUNTABLE

Have you ever wished you could look over a Bible translator's shoulder as he or she worked?

Bible translation usually happens behind closed doors—few outside the translation committee see the complex decisions underlying the words that appear in their English Bibles. Fewer still have the opportunity to review and speak into the translators' decisions.

Throughout the NET's translation process, every working draft was made publicly available on the Internet. Bible scholars, ministers, and laypersons from around the world logged millions of review sessions. No other translation is so openly accountable to the worldwide church or has been so thoroughly vetted.

And yet the ultimate accountability was to the biblical text itself. The NET Bible is neither crowdsourced nor a "translation by consensus." Rather, the NET translators filtered every question and suggestion through the very best insights from biblical linguistics, textual criticism, and their unswerving commitment to following the text wherever it leads. Thus, the NET remains supremely accurate and trustworthy while also benefiting from extensive review by those who would be reading, studying, and teaching from its pages.

BEYOND THE "READABLE VS. ACCURATE" DIVIDE

The uniquely transparent and accountable translation process of the NET has been crystallized in the most extensive set of Bible translators' notes ever created. More than 60,000 notes highlight every major decision, outline alternative views, and explain difficult or nontraditional renderings. Freely available at netbible.org and in print in the *NET Bible, Full Notes Edition*, these notes help the NET overcome one of the biggest challenges facing any Bible translation: the tension between *accuracy* and *readability*.

If you have spent more than a few minutes researching the English version of the Bible, you have probably encountered a "translation spectrum"—a simple chart with the most wooden-but-precise translations and paraphrases on the far left (representing a "word-for-word" translation approach) and the loosest-but-easiest-to-read translations and paraphrases on the far right (representing a "thought-for-thought" philosophy of translation). Some translations intentionally lean toward one end of the spectrum or the other, embracing the strengths and weaknesses of their chosen approach. Most try to strike a balance between the extremes, weighing accuracy against readability—striving to reflect the grammar of the underlying biblical languages while still achieving acceptable English style.

But the NET moves beyond that old dichotomy. Because of the extensive translators' notes, the NET never has to compromise. Whenever faced with a difficult translation choice, the translators were free to put the strongest option in the main text while documenting the challenge, their thought process, and the solution in the notes.

The benefit to you, the reader? You can be sure that the NET is a translation you can trust—nothing has been lost in translation or obscured by a translator's dilemma. Instead, you are invited to see for yourself and gain the kind of transparent access to the biblical languages previously available only to scholars.

MINISTRY FIRST

One more reason to love the NET: Modern Bible translations are typically copyrighted, posing a challenge for ministries hoping to quote more than a few passages in their Bible study resources, curriculum, or other programming. But the NET is for everyone, with "ministry first" copyright innovations that encourage ministries to quote and share the life-changing message of Scripture as freely as possible. In fact, one of the major motivations behind the creation of the NET was the desire to ensure that ministries had un-fettered access to a top-quality modern Bible translation without needing to embark on a complicated process of securing permissions.

Visit netbible.com/net-bible-copyright to learn more.

TAKE UP AND READ

With its balanced, easy-to-understand En-glish text and a transparent translation pro-cess that invites you to see for yourself the richness of the biblical languages, the NET is a Bible you can embrace as your own. Clear, read-able, elegant, and accurate, the NET presents Scripture as meaningfully and powerfully to-day as when these words were first communi-cated to the people of God.

Our prayer is that the NET will be a fresh and exciting invitation to you—and Bible readers everywhere—to "let the word of Christ dwell in you richly" (Col 3:16).

The Publishers

ROMANS

PROLOGUE

Rome had always been in Paul's plans. Each missionary effort pushed him farther in that direction, yet he had not even set foot on the Italian peninsula. But he would keep trying. It was too important. Rome was the gateway to the rest of the world. If the gospel were to saturate that city, it would speed fulfilling the assignment Jesus had given to his church. But spreading the right gospel—the *true* gospel—was critical. False gospels had already arisen, leading to confusion and error.

Paul was now on his third missionary journey, and he could wait no longer. He had to ensure that the church in Rome was being built on the solid foundation of the true gospel rather than the shaky, crumbling foundation of error. Paul decided to write a letter to the church in Rome, then follow with a visit.

Not only did the believers need to know what the gospel was, they needed to know how it worked. If everyone sinned, why was God angry? How could God be righteous and yet forgive people? To answer these questions Paul would point to Jesus, of course, but not just him. Paul would take his readers back to Abraham and even earlier, to the creation of the world. The answers to their questions began there.

CHAPTER 1

SALUTATION

From Paul, a slave of Christ Jesus, called to be an apostle, set apart for the gospel of God. This gospel he promised beforehand through his prophets in the holy scriptures, concerning his Son who was a descendant of David with reference to the flesh, who was appointed the Son-of-God-in-power according to the Holy Spirit by the resurrection from the dead, Jesus Christ our Lord. Through him we have received grace and our apostleship to bring about the obedience of faith among all the Gentiles on behalf of his name. You also are among them, called to belong to Jesus Christ. To all those loved by God in Rome, called to be saints: Grace and peace to you from God our Father and the Lord Jesus Christ!

PAUL'S DESIRE TO VISIT ROME

First of all, I thank my God through Jesus Christ for all of you, because your faith is proclaimed throughout the whole world. For God, whom I serve in my spirit in the gospel of his Son, is my witness that I continually remember you, and I always ask in my prayers if, perhaps now at last, I may succeed in visiting you according to the will of God. For I long to see you, so that I may impart to you some spiritual gift to strengthen you, that is, that we may be mutually comforted by one another's faith, both yours and mine. I do not want you to be unaware, brothers and sisters, that I often intended to come to you (and was prevented until now), so that I may have some fruit even among you, just as I already have among the rest of the Gentiles. I am a debtor both to the Greeks and to the barbarians, both to the wise and to the foolish. Thus I am eager also to preach the gospel to you who are in Rome.

THE POWER OF THE GOSPEL

For I am not ashamed of the gospel, for it is God's power for salvation to everyone who believes, to the Jew first and also to the Greek. For the righteousness of God is revealed in the gospel from faith to faith, just as it is written, *"The righteous by faith will live."*

THE CONDEMNATION OF THE UNRIGHTEOUS

For the wrath of God is revealed from heaven against all ungodliness and unrighteousness of people who suppress the truth by their unrighteousness, because what can be known about God is plain to them, because God has made it plain to them. For since the creation of the world his invisible attributes—his eternal power and divine nature—have been clearly seen because they are understood through what has been made. So people are without excuse. For although they knew God, they did not glorify him as God or give him thanks, but they became futile in their thoughts, and their senseless hearts were darkened. Although they claimed to be wise, they became fools and exchanged the glory of the immortal God for an image resembling mortal human beings or birds or four-footed animals or reptiles.

Therefore God gave them over in the desires of their hearts to impurity, to dishonor their bodies among themselves. They exchanged the truth of God for a lie and worshiped and served the creation rather than the Creator, who is blessed forever! Amen.

For this reason God gave them over to dishonorable passions. For their women exchanged the natural sexual relations for unnatural ones, and likewise the men also abandoned natural relations with women and were inflamed in their passions for one another. Men committed shameless acts with men and received in themselves the due penalty for their error.

And just as they did not see fit to acknowledge God, God gave them over to a depraved mind, to do what should not be done. They are filled with every kind of unrighteousness, wickedness, covetousness, malice. They are rife with envy, murder, strife, deceit, hostility. They are gossips, slanderers, haters of God, insolent, arrogant, boastful, contrivers of all sorts of evil, disobedient to parents, sense- less, covenant-breakers, heartless, ruthless. Although they fully know God's righteous de- cree that those who practice such things de- serve to die, they not only do them but also approve of those who practice them.

CHAPTER 2

THE CONDEMNATION OF THE MORALIST

Therefore you are without excuse, whoever you are, when you judge someone else. For on whatever grounds you judge another, you con- demn yourself, because you who judge practice the same things. Now we know that God's judg- ment is in accordance with truth against those who practice such things. And do you think, whoever you are, when you judge those who practice such things and yet do them yourself, that you will escape God's judgment? Or do you have contempt for the wealth of his kind- ness, forbearance, and patience, and yet do not know that God's kindness leads you to repen- tance? But because of your stubbornness and your unrepentant heart, you are storing up wrath for yourselves in the day of wrath, when God's righteous judgment is revealed! He *will reward each one according to his works*: eter- nal life to those who by perseverance in good works seek glory and honor and immortality, but wrath and anger to those who live in selfish ambition and do not obey the truth but follow unrighteousness. There will be affliction and distress on everyone who does evil, on the Jew first and also the Greek, but glory and honor and peace for everyone who does good, for the Jew first and also the Greek. For there is no partiality with God. For all who have sinned apart from the law will also perish apart from the law, and all who have sinned under the law will be judged by the law. For it is not those who hear the law who are righteous before God, but those who do the law will be declared righteous. For whenever the Gentiles, who do not have the law, do by nature the things required by the law, these who do not have the law are a law to themselves. They show that the work of the law is written in their hearts, as their conscience bears witness and their conflicting thoughts accuse or else defend them, on the day when God will judge the secrets of human hearts, according to my gospel through Christ Jesus.

THE CONDEMNATION OF THE JEW

But if you call yourself a Jew and rely on the law and boast of your relationship to God and know his will and approve the superior things because you receive instruction from the law, and if you are convinced that you yourself are a guide to the blind, a light to those who are in darkness, an educator of the senseless, a teacher of little children, because you have in the law the essential features of knowledge and of the truth—therefore you who teach someone else, do you not teach yourself? You who preach against stealing, do you steal? You who tell others not to commit adultery, do you commit adultery? You who abhor idols, do you rob temples? You who boast in the law dishonor God by transgressing the law! For just as it is written, *"the name of God is being blasphemed among the Gentiles because of you."*

For circumcision has its value if you practice the law, but if you break the law, your circumcision has become uncircumcision. Therefore if the uncircumcised man obeys the righteous requirements of the law, will not his uncircumcision be regarded as circumcision? And the physically uncircumcised man, by keeping the law, will judge you to be the transgressor of the law, even though you have the letter and circumcision! For a person is not a Jew who is one outwardly, nor is circumcision something that is outward in the flesh, but someone is a Jew who is one inwardly, and circumcision is of the heart by the Spirit and not by the letter. This person's praise is not from people but from God.

CHAPTER 3

Therefore what advantage does the Jew have, or what is the value of circumcision? Actually, there are many advantages. First of all, the Jews were entrusted with the oracles of God. What then? If some were unfaithful, their unfaithfulness will not nullify God's faithfulness, will it? Absolutely not! Let God be proven true, and every human being shown up as a liar, just as it is written: *"so that you will be justified in your words and will prevail when you are judged."*

But if our unrighteousness demonstrates the righteousness of God, what shall we say? The God who inflicts wrath is not unrighteous, is he? (I am speaking in human terms.) Absolutely not! For otherwise how could God judge the world? For if by my lie the truth of God enhances his glory, why am I still actually being judged as a sinner? And why not say, "Let us do evil so that good may come of it"?—as some who slander us allege that we say. (Their condemnation is deserved!)

THE CONDEMNATION OF THE WORLD

What then? Are we better off? Certainly not, for we have already charged that Jews and Greeks alike are all under sin, just as it is written:

"There is no one righteous, not even one;
there is no one who understands;
there is no one who seeks God.
All have turned away;
together they have become worthless;
there is no one who shows kindness, not
    even one."

"Their throats are open graves;
they deceive with their tongues;
the poison of asps is under their lips."
"Their mouths are full of cursing and
* bitterness."*
"Their feet are swift to shed blood;
ruin and misery are in their paths,
and the way of peace they have not known."
"There is no fear of God before their eyes."

Now we know that whatever the law says, it says to those who are under the law, so that every mouth may be silenced and the whole world may be held accountable to God. For *no one is declared righteous before him* by the works of the law, for through the law comes the knowledge of sin. But now apart from the law the righteousness of God (although it is attested by the law and the prophets) has been disclosed—namely, the righteousness of God through the faithfulness of Jesus Christ for all who believe. For there is no distinction, for all have sinned and fall short of the glory of God. But they are justified freely by his grace through the redemption that is in Christ Jesus. God publicly displayed him at his death as the mercy seat accessible through faith. This was to demonstrate his righteousness because God in his forbearance had passed over the sins previously committed. This was also to demonstrate his righteousness in the present time, so that he would be just and the justifier of the one who lives because of Jesus' faithfulness.

Where, then, is boasting? It is excluded! By what principle? Of works? No, but by the principle of faith! For we consider that a person is declared righteous by faith apart from the works of the law. Or is God the God of the Jews only? Is he not the God of the Gentiles too? Yes, of the Gentiles too! Since God is one, he will justify the circumcised by faith and the uncircumcised through faith. Do we then nullify the law through faith? Absolutely not! Instead we uphold the law.

CHAPTER 4

THE ILLUSTRATION OF JUSTIFICATION

What then shall we say that Abraham, our ancestor according to the flesh, has discovered regarding this matter? For if Abraham was declared righteous by works, he has something to boast about—but not before God. For what does the scripture say? *"Abraham believed God, and it was credited to him as righteousness."* Now to the one who works, his pay is not credited due to grace but due to obligation. But to the one who does not work, but believes in the one who declares the ungodly righteous, his faith is credited as righteousness.

So even David himself speaks regarding the blessedness of the man to whom God credits righteousness apart from works:

> *"Blessed are those whose lawless deeds are forgiven, and whose sins are covered; blessed is the one against whom the Lord will never count sin."*

Is this blessedness then for the circumcision or also for the uncircumcision? For we say, "faith **was credited to** Abraham **as righteousness.**" How then was it credited to him? Was he circumcised at the time, or not? No, he was not circumcised but uncircumcised! And he received the sign of circumcision as a seal of the righteousness that he had by faith while he was still uncircumcised, so that he would become the father of all those who believe but have never been circumcised, that they too could have righteousness credited to them. And he is also the father of the circumcised, who are not only circumcised, but who also walk in the footsteps of the faith that our father Abraham possessed when he was still uncircumcised.

For the promise to Abraham or to his descendants that he would inherit the world was not fulfilled through the law, but through the righteousness that comes by faith. For if they become heirs by the law, faith is empty and the promise is nullified. For the law brings wrath, because where there is no law there is no transgression either. For this reason it is by faith so that it may be by grace, with the result that the promise may be certain to all the descendants—not only to those who are under the law, but also to those who have the faith of Abraham, who is the father of us all (as it is written, "*I have made you the father of many nations*"). He is our father in the presence of God whom he believed—the God who makes the dead alive and summons the things that do not yet exist as though they already do. Against hope Abraham believed in hope with the result that he became *the father of many nations* according to the pronouncement, "*so will your descendants be.*" Without being weak in faith, he considered his own body as dead (because he was about one hundred years old) and the deadness of Sarah's womb. He did not waver in unbelief about the promise of God but was strengthened in faith, giving glory to God. He was fully convinced that what God promised he was also able to do. So indeed it was credited to Abraham as righteousness.

But the statement *it was credited to him* was not written only for Abraham's sake, but also for our sake, to whom it will be credited, those who believe in the one who raised Jesus our Lord from the dead. He was given over because of our transgressions and was raised for the sake of our justification.

CHAPTER 5

THE EXPECTATION OF JUSTIFICATION

Therefore, since we have been declared righteous by faith, we have peace with God through our Lord Jesus Christ, through whom we have also obtained access into this grace in which we stand, and we rejoice in the hope of God's glory. Not only this, but we also rejoice in sufferings, knowing that suffering produces endurance, and endurance, character, and character, hope. And hope does not disappoint, because the love of God has been poured out in our hearts through the Holy Spirit who was given to us.

For while we were still helpless, at the right time Christ died for the ungodly. (For rarely will anyone die for a righteous person, though for a good person perhaps someone might possibly dare to die.) But God demonstrates his own love for us, in that while we were still sinners, Christ died for us. Much more then, because we have now been declared righteous by his blood, we will be saved through him from God's wrath. For if while we were enemies we were reconciled to God through the death of his Son, how much more, since we have been reconciled, will we be saved by his life? Not only this, but we also rejoice in God through our Lord Jesus Christ, through whom we have now received this reconciliation.

THE AMPLIFICATION OF JUSTIFICATION

So then, just as sin entered the world through one man and death through sin, and so death spread to all people because all sinned—for before the law was given, sin was in the world, but there is no accounting for sin when there is no law. Yet death reigned from Adam until Moses even over those who did not sin in the same way that Adam (who is a type of the coming one) transgressed. But the gracious gift is not like the transgression. For if the many died through the transgression of the one man, how much more did the grace of God and the gift by the grace of the one man Jesus Christ multiply to the many! And the gift is not like the one who sinned. For judgment, resulting from the one transgression, led to condemnation, but the gracious gift from the many failures led to justification. For if, by the transgression of the one man, death reigned through the one, how much more will those who receive the abundance of grace and of the gift of righteousness reign in life through the one, Jesus Christ!

Consequently, just as condemnation for all people came through one transgression, so too through the one righteous act came righteousness leading to life for all people. For just as through the disobedience of the one man many were constituted sinners, so also through the obedience of one man many will be constituted righteous. Now the law came in so that the transgression may increase, but where sin increased, grace multiplied all the more, so that just as sin reigned in death, so also grace will reign through righteousness to eternal life through Jesus Christ our Lord.

CHAPTER 6

THE BELIEVER'S FREEDOM
FROM SIN'S DOMINATION

What shall we say then? Are we to remain in sin so that grace may increase? Absolutely not! How can we who died to sin still live in it? Or do you not know that as many as were baptized into Christ Jesus were baptized into his death? Therefore we have been buried with him through baptism into death, in order that just as Christ was raised from the dead through the glory of the Father, so we too may live a new life.

For if we have become united with him in the likeness of his death, we will certainly also be united in the likeness of his resurrection. We know that our old man was crucified with him so that the body of sin would no longer dominate us, so that we would no longer be enslaved to sin. (For someone who has died has been freed from sin.)

Now if we died with Christ, we believe that we will also live with him. We know that since Christ has been raised from the dead, he is never going to die again; death no longer has mastery over him. For the death he died, he died to sin once for all, but the life he lives, he lives to God. So you too consider yourselves dead to sin, but alive to God in Christ Jesus.

Therefore do not let sin reign in your mortal body so that you obey its desires, and do not present your members to sin as instruments to be used for unrighteousness, but present yourselves to God as those who are alive from the dead and your members to God as instruments to be used for righteousness. For sin will have no mastery over you, because you are not under law but under grace.

THE BELIEVER'S ENSLAVEMENT TO GOD'S RIGHTEOUSNESS

What then? Shall we sin because we are not under law but under grace? Absolutely not! Do you not know that if you present yourselves as obedient slaves, you are slaves of the one you obey, either of sin resulting in death, or obedience resulting in righteousness? But thanks be to God that though you were slaves to sin, you obeyed from the heart that pattern of teaching you were entrusted to, and having been freed from sin, you became enslaved to righteousness. (I am speaking in human terms because of the weakness of your flesh.) For just as you once presented your members as slaves to impurity and lawlessness leading to more lawlessness, so now present your members as slaves to righteousness leading to sanctification. For when you were slaves of sin, you were free with regard to righteousness.

So what benefit did you then reap from those things that you are now ashamed of? For the end of those things is death. But now, freed from sin and enslaved to God, you have your benefit leading to sanctification, and the end is eternal life. For the payoff of sin is death, but the gift of God is eternal life in Christ Jesus our Lord.

CHAPTER 7

THE BELIEVER'S RELATIONSHIP TO THE LAW

Or do you not know, brothers and sisters (for I am speaking to those who know the law), that the law is lord over a person as long as he lives? For a married woman is bound by law to her husband as long as he lives, but if her husband dies, she is released from the law of the marriage. So then, if she is joined to another man while her husband is alive, she will be called an adulteress. But if her husband dies, she is free from that law, and if she is joined to another man, she is not an adulteress. So, my brothers and sisters, you also died to the law through the body of Christ, so that you could be joined to another, to the one who was raised from the dead, to bear fruit to God. For when we were in the flesh, the sinful desires, aroused by the law, were active in the members of our body to bear fruit for death. But now we have been released from the law, because we have died to what controlled us, so that we may serve in the new life of the Spirit and not under the old written code.

What shall we say then? Is the law sin? Absolutely not! Certainly, I would not have known sin except through the law. For indeed I would not have known what it means to desire something belonging to someone else if the law had not said, *"Do not covet."* But sin, seizing the opportunity through the commandment, produced in me all kinds of wrong desires. For apart from the law, sin is dead. And I was once alive apart from the law, but with the coming of the commandment, sin became alive and I died. So I found that the very commandment that was intended to bring life brought death! For sin, seizing the opportunity through the commandment, deceived me and through it I died. So then, the law is holy, and the commandment is holy, righteous, and good.

Did that which is good, then, become death to me? Absolutely not! But sin, so that it would be shown to be sin, produced death in me through what is good, so that through the commandment sin would become utterly sinful. For we know that the law is spiritual—but I am unspiritual, sold into slavery to sin. For I don't understand what I am doing. For I do not do what I want—instead, I do what I hate. But if I do what I don't want, I agree that the law is good. But now it is no longer me doing it, but sin that lives in me. For I know that nothing good lives in me, that is, in my flesh. For I want to do the good, but I cannot do it. For I do not do the good I want, but I do the very evil I do not want! Now if I do what I do not want, it is no longer me doing it but sin that lives in me.

So, I find the law that when I want to do good, evil is present with me. For I delight in the law of God in my inner being. But I see a different law in my members waging war against the law of my mind and making me captive to the law of sin that is in my members. Wretched man that I am! Who will rescue me from this body of death? Thanks be to God through Jesus Christ our Lord! So then, I myself serve the law of God with my mind, but with my flesh I serve the law of sin.

CHAPTER 8

THE BELIEVER'S RELATIONSHIP TO THE HOLY SPIRIT

There is therefore now no condemnation for those who are in Christ Jesus. For the law of the life-giving Spirit in Christ Jesus has set you free from the law of sin and death. For God achieved what the law could not do because it was weakened through the flesh. By sending his own Son in the likeness of sinful flesh and concerning sin, he condemned sin in the flesh, so that the righteous requirement of the law may be fulfilled in us, who do not walk according to the flesh but according to the Spirit.

For those who live according to the flesh have their outlook shaped by the things of the flesh, but those who live according to the Spirit have their outlook shaped by the things of the Spirit. For the outlook of the flesh is death, but the outlook of the Spirit is life and peace, because the outlook of the flesh is hostile to God, for it does not submit to the law of God, nor is it able to do so. Those who are in the flesh cannot please God. You, however, are not in the flesh but in the Spirit, if indeed the Spirit of God lives in you. Now if anyone does not have the Spirit of Christ, this person does not belong to him. But if Christ is in you, your body is dead because of sin, but the Spirit is your life because of righteousness. Moreover if the Spirit of the one who raised Jesus from the dead lives in you, the one who raised Christ from the dead will also make your mortal bodies alive through his Spirit who lives in you.

So then, brothers and sisters, we are under obligation, not to the flesh, to live according to the flesh (for if you live according to the flesh, you will die), but if by the Spirit you put to death the deeds of the body, you will live. For all who are led by the Spirit of God are the sons of God. For you did not receive the spirit of slavery leading again to fear, but you received the Spirit of adoption, by whom we cry, "*Abba,* Father." The Spirit himself bears witness to our spirit that we are God's children. And if children, then heirs (namely, heirs of God and also fellow heirs with Christ)—if indeed we suffer with him so we may also be glorified with him.

For I consider that our present sufferings cannot even be compared to the coming glory that will be revealed to us. For the creation eagerly waits for the revelation of the sons of God. For the creation was subjected to futility—not willingly but because of God who subjected it—in hope that the creation itself will also be set free from the bondage of decay into the glorious freedom of God's children. For we know that the whole creation groans and suffers together until now. Not only this, but we ourselves also, who have the firstfruits of the Spirit, groan inwardly as we eagerly await our adoption, the redemption of our bodies. For in hope we were saved. Now hope that is seen is not hope, because who hopes for what he sees? But if we hope for what we do not see, we eagerly wait for it with endurance.

In the same way, the Spirit helps us in our weakness, for we do not know how we should pray, but the Spirit himself intercedes for us with inexpressible groanings. And he who searches our hearts knows the mind of the Spirit, because the Spirit intercedes on behalf of the saints according to God's will. And we know that all things work together for good for those who love God, who are called according to his purpose, because those whom he foreknew he also predestined to be conformed to the image of his Son, that his Son would be the firstborn among many brothers and sisters. And those he predestined, he also called; and those he called, he also justified; and those he justified, he also glorified.

What then shall we say about these things? If God is for us, who can be against us? Indeed, he who did not spare his own Son, but gave him up for us all—how will he not also, along with him, freely give us all things? Who will bring any charge against God's elect? It is God who justifies. Who is the one who will condemn? Christ is the one who died (and more than that, he was raised), who is at the right hand of God, and who also is interceding for us. Who will separate us from the love of Christ? Will trouble, or distress, or persecution, or famine, or nakedness, or danger, or sword? As it is written, *"For your sake we encounter death all day long; we were considered as sheep to be slaughtered."* No, in all these things we have complete victory through him who loved us! For I am convinced that neither death, nor life, nor angels, nor heavenly rulers, nor things that are present, nor things to come, nor powers, nor height, nor depth, nor anything else in creation will be able to separate us from the love of God in Christ Jesus our Lord.

CHAPTER 9

ISRAEL'S REJECTION CONSIDERED

I am telling the truth in Christ (I am not lying!), for my conscience assures me in the Holy Spirit—I have great sorrow and unceasing anguish in my heart. For I could wish that I myself were accursed—cut off from

Christ—for the sake of my people, my fellow countrymen, who are Israelites. To them belong the adoption as sons, the glory, the covenants, the giving of the law, the temple worship, and the promises. To them belong the patriarchs, and from them, by human descent, came the Christ, who is God over all, blessed forever! Amen.

It is not as though the word of God had failed. For not all those who are descended from Israel are truly Israel, nor are all the children Abraham's true descendants; rather "*through Isaac will your descendants be counted.*" This means it is not the children of the flesh who are the children of God; rather, the children of promise are counted as descendants. For this is what the promise declared: "*About a year from now I will return and Sarah will have a son.*" Not only that, but when Rebekah had conceived children by one man, our ancestor Isaac—even before they were born or had done anything good or bad (so that God's purpose in election would stand, not by works but by his calling)—it was said to her, "*The older will serve the younger,*" just as it is written: "*Jacob I loved, but Esau I hated.*"

What shall we say then? Is there injustice with God? Absolutely not! For he says to Moses: "*I will have mercy on whom I have mercy, and I will have compassion on whom I have compassion.*" So then, it does not depend on human desire or exertion, but on God who shows mercy. For the scripture says to Pharaoh: *"For this very purpose I have raised you up, that I may demonstrate my power in you, and that my name may be proclaimed in all the earth."* So then, God has mercy on whom he chooses to have mercy, and he hardens whom he chooses to harden.

You will say to me then, "Why does he still find fault? For who has ever resisted his will?" But who indeed are you—a mere human being—to talk back to God? *Does what is molded say to the molder, "Why have you made me like this?"* Has the potter no right to make from the same lump of clay one vessel for special use and another for ordinary use? But what if God, willing to demonstrate his wrath and to make known his power, has endured with much patience the objects of wrath prepared for destruction? And what if he is willing to make known the wealth of his glory on the objects of mercy that he has prepared beforehand for glory—even us, whom he has called, not only from the Jews but also from the Gentiles? As he also says in Hosea:

> *"I will call those who were not my people,*
> *'My people,' and I will call her who was*
> *unloved, 'My beloved.' "*
> *"And in the very place where it was said to*
> *them, 'You are not my people,'*
> *there they will be called 'sons of the*
> *living God.' "*

And Isaiah cries out on behalf of Israel, *"Though the number of the children of Israel are as the sand of the sea, only the remnant will be saved, for the Lord will execute his sentence on the earth completely and quickly."* Just as Isaiah predicted,

> *"If the Lord of Heaven's Armies had not left us descendants,*
> *we would have become like Sodom,*
> *and we would have resembled Gomorrah."*

ISRAEL'S REJECTION CULPABLE

What shall we say then?—that the Gentiles who did not pursue righteousness obtained it, that is, a righteousness that is by faith, but Israel even though pursuing a law of righteousness did not attain it. Why not? Because they pursued it not by faith but (as if it were possible) by works. They stumbled over the stumbling stone, just as it is written,

> *"Look, I am laying in Zion a stone that will cause people to stumble*
> *and a rock that will make them fall,*
> *yet the one who believes in him will not be put to shame."*

CHAPTER 10

Brothers and sisters, my heart's desire and prayer to God on behalf of my fellow Israelites is for their salvation. For I can testify that they are zealous for God, but their zeal is not in line with the truth. For ignoring the righteousness that comes from God and seeking instead to establish their own righteousness, they did not submit to God's righteousness. For Christ is the end of the law, with the result that there is righteousness for everyone who believes.

For Moses writes about the righteousness that is by the law: *"The one who does these things will live by them."* But the righteousness that is by faith says: *"Do not say in your heart, 'Who will ascend into heaven?'"* (that is, to bring Christ down) or *"Who will descend into the abyss?"* (that is, to bring Christ up from the dead). But what does it say? *"The word is near you, in your mouth and in your heart"* (that is, the word of faith that we preach), because if you confess with your mouth that Jesus is Lord and believe in your heart that God raised him from the dead, you will be saved. For with the heart one believes and thus has righteousness and with the mouth one confesses and thus has salvation. For the scripture says, *"Everyone who believes in him will not be put to shame."* For there is no distinction between the Jew and the Greek, for the same Lord is Lord of all, who richly blesses all who call on him. For *everyone who calls on the name of the Lord will be saved.*

How are they to call on one they have not believed in? And how are they to believe in one they have not heard of? And how are they to hear without someone preaching to them? And how are they to preach unless they are sent? As it is written, *"How timely is the arrival of those who proclaim the good news."* But not all have obeyed the good news, for

Isaiah says, "**Lord, who has believed our report?**" Consequently faith comes from what is heard, and what is heard comes through the preached word of Christ.

But I ask, have they not heard? Yes, they have: *Their voice has gone out to all the earth, and their words to the ends of the world.* But again I ask, didn't Israel understand? First Moses says, "*I will make you jealous by those who are not a nation; with a senseless nation I will provoke you to anger.*" And Isaiah is even bold enough to say, "*I was found by those who did not seek me; I became well known to those who did not ask for me.*" But about Israel he says, "*All day long I held out my hands to this disobedient and stubborn people!*"

CHAPTER 11

ISRAEL'S REJECTION NOT COMPLETE NOR FINAL

So I ask, God has not rejected his people, has he? Absolutely not! For I too am an Israelite, a descendant of Abraham, from the tribe of Benjamin. God has not rejected his people whom he foreknew! Do you not know what the scripture says about Elijah, how he pleads with God against Israel? "Lord, *they have killed your prophets; they have demolished your altars; I alone am left, and they are seeking my life!*" But what was the divine response to him? "*I have kept for myself 7,000 people who have not bent the knee to Baal.*"

So in the same way at the present time there is a remnant chosen by grace. And if it is by grace, it is no longer by works, otherwise grace would no longer be grace. What then? Israel failed to obtain what it was diligently seeking, but the elect obtained it. The rest were hardened, as it is written,

"God gave them a spirit of stupor,
eyes that would not see and ears that
*   would not hear,*
to this very day."

And David says,

"Let their table become a snare and trap,
a stumbling block and a retribution for
*   them;*
let their eyes be darkened so that they may
*   not see,*
and make their backs bend continually."

I ask then, they did not stumble into an irrevocable fall, did they? Absolutely not! But by their transgression salvation has come to the Gentiles, to make Israel jealous. Now if their transgression means riches for the world and their defeat means riches for the Gentiles, how much more will their full restoration bring?

Now I am speaking to you Gentiles. Seeing that I am an apostle to the Gentiles, I magnify my ministry, if somehow I could provoke my people to jealousy and save some of them. For if their rejection is the reconciliation of the world, what will their acceptance be but life from the dead? If the first portion of the dough offered is holy, then the whole batch is holy, and if the root is holy, so too are the branches.

Now if some of the branches were broken off, and you, a wild olive shoot, were grafted in among them and participated in the richness of the olive root, do not boast over the branches. But if you boast, remember that you do not support the root, but the root supports you. Then you will say, "The branches were broken off so that I could be grafted in." Granted! They were broken off because of their unbelief, but you stand by faith. Do not be arrogant, but fear! For if God did not spare the natural branches, perhaps he will not spare you. Notice therefore the kindness and harshness of God—harshness toward those who have fallen, but God's kindness toward you, provided you continue in his kindness; otherwise you also will be cut off. And even they—if they do not continue in their unbelief—will be grafted in, for God is able to graft them in again. For if you were cut off from what is by nature a wild olive tree, and grafted, contrary to nature, into a cultivated olive tree, how much more will these natural branches be grafted back into their own olive tree?

For I do not want you to be ignorant of this mystery, brothers and sisters, so that you may not be conceited: A partial hardening has happened to Israel until the full number of the Gentiles has come in. And so all Israel will be saved, as it is written:

"The Deliverer will come out of Zion;
he will remove ungodliness from Jacob.
And this is my covenant with them,
when I take away their sins."

In regard to the gospel they are enemies for your sake, but in regard to election they are dearly loved for the sake of the fathers. For the gifts and the call of God are irrevocable. Just as you were formerly disobedient to God, but have now received mercy due to their disobedience, so they too have now been disobedient in order that, by the mercy shown to you, they too may now receive mercy. For God has consigned all people to disobedience so that he may show mercy to them all.

Oh, the depth of the riches and wisdom and knowledge of God! How unsearchable are his judgments and how unfathomable his ways!

For who has known the mind of the Lord,
or who has been his counselor?
Or who has first given to God
that God needs to repay him?

For from him and through him and to him are all things. To him be glory forever! Amen.

CHAPTER 12

CONSECRATION OF THE BELIEVER'S LIFE

Therefore I exhort you, brothers and sisters, by the mercies of God, to present your bodies as a sacrifice—alive, holy, and pleasing to God—which is your reasonable service. Do not be conformed to this present world, but be transformed by the renewing of your mind, so that you may test and approve what is the will of God—what is good and well-pleasing and perfect.

CONDUCT IN HUMILITY

For by the grace given to me I say to every one of you not to think more highly of yourself than you ought to think, but to think with sober discernment, as God has distributed to each of you a measure of faith. For just as in one body we have many members, and not all the members serve the same function, so we who are many are one body in Christ, and individually we are members who belong to one another. And we have different gifts according to the grace given to us. If the gift is prophecy, that individual must use it in proportion to his faith. If it is service, he must serve; if it is teaching, he must teach; if it is exhortation, he must exhort; if it is contributing, he must do so with sincerity; if it is leadership, he must do so with diligence; if it is showing mercy, he must do so with cheerfulness.

CONDUCT IN LOVE

Love must be without hypocrisy. Abhor what is evil, cling to what is good. Be devoted to one another with mutual love, showing eagerness in honoring one another. Do not lag in zeal, be enthusiastic in spirit, serve the Lord. Rejoice in hope, endure in suffering, persist in prayer. Contribute to the needs of the saints, pursue hospitality. Bless those who persecute you, bless and do not curse. Rejoice with those who rejoice, weep with those who weep. Live in harmony with one another; do not be haughty but associate with the lowly. Do not be conceited. Do not repay anyone evil for evil; consider what is good before all people. If possible, so far as it depends on you, live peaceably with all people. Do not avenge yourselves, dear friends, but give place to God's wrath, for it is written, *"Vengeance is mine, I will repay,"* says the Lord. Rather, *if your enemy is hungry, feed him; if he is thirsty, give him a drink; for in doing this you will be heaping burning coals on his head.* Do not be overcome by evil, but overcome evil with good.

CHAPTER 13

SUBMISSION TO CIVIL GOVERNMENT

Let every person be subject to the governing authorities. For there is no authority except by God's appointment, and the authorities that exist have been instituted by God. So the person who resists such authority resists the ordinance of God, and those who resist will incur judgment (for rulers cause no fear for good conduct but for bad).

Do you desire not to fear authority? Do good and you will receive its commendation because it is God's servant for your well-being. But be afraid if you do wrong because government does not bear the sword for nothing. It is God's servant to administer punishment on the person who does wrong. Therefore it is necessary to be in subjection, not only because of the wrath of the authorities but also because of your conscience. For this reason you also pay taxes, for the authorities are God's servants devoted to governing. Pay everyone what is owed: taxes to whom taxes are due, revenue to whom revenue is due, respect to whom respect is due, honor to whom honor is due.

EXHORTATION TO LOVE NEIGHBORS

Owe no one anything, except to love one another, for the one who loves his neighbor has fulfilled the law. For the commandments, *"Do not commit adultery, do not murder, do not steal, do not covet,"* (and if there is any other commandment) are summed up in this, *"Love your neighbor as yourself."* Love does no wrong to a neighbor. Therefore love is the fulfillment of the law.

MOTIVATION TO GODLY CONDUCT

And do this because we know the time, that it is already the hour for us to awake from sleep, for our salvation is now nearer than when we became believers. The night has advanced toward dawn; the day is near. So then we must lay aside the works of darkness, and put on the weapons of light. Let us live decently as in the daytime, not in carousing and drunkenness, not in sexual immorality and sensuality, not in discord and jealousy. Instead, put on the Lord Jesus Christ, and make no provision for the flesh to arouse its desires.

CHAPTER 14

EXHORTATION TO MUTUAL FORBEARANCE

Now receive the one who is weak in the faith, and do not have disputes over differing opinions. One person believes in eating everything, but the weak person eats only vegetables. The one who eats everything must not despise the one who does not, and the one who abstains must not judge the one who eats everything, for God has accepted him. Who are you to pass judgment on another's servant? Before his own master he stands or falls. And he will stand, for the Lord is able to make him stand.

One person regards one day holier than other days, and another regards them all alike. Each must be fully convinced in his own mind. The one who observes the day does it for the Lord. The one who eats, eats for the Lord because he gives thanks to God, and the one who abstains from eating abstains for the Lord, and he gives thanks to God. For none of us lives for himself and none dies for himself. If we live, we live for the Lord; if we die, we die for the Lord. Therefore, whether we live or die, we are the Lord's. For this reason Christ died and returned to life, so that he may be the Lord of both the dead and the living.

But you who eat vegetables only—why do you judge your brother or sister? And you who eat everything—why do you despise your brother or sister? For we will all stand before the judgment seat of God. For it is written, "*As I live, says the Lord, every knee will bow to me, and every tongue will give praise to God.*" Therefore, each of us will give an account of himself to God.

**EXHORTATION FOR THE STRONG
NOT TO DESTROY THE WEAK**

Therefore we must not pass judgment on one another, but rather determine never to place an obstacle or a trap before a brother or sister. I know and am convinced in the Lord Jesus that there is nothing unclean in itself; still, it is unclean to the one who considers it unclean. For if your brother or sister is distressed because of what you eat, you are no longer walking in love. Do not destroy by your food someone for whom Christ died. Therefore do not let what you consider good be spoken of as evil. For the kingdom of God does not consist of food and drink, but righteousness, peace, and joy in the Holy Spirit. For the one who serves Christ in this way is pleasing to God and approved by people.

So then, let us pursue what makes for peace and for building up one another. Do not destroy the work of God for the sake of food. For although all things are clean, it is wrong to cause anyone to stumble by what you eat. It is good not to eat meat or drink wine or to do anything that causes your brother to stumble. The faith you have, keep to yourself before God. Blessed is the one who does not judge himself by what he approves. But the man who doubts is condemned if he eats, because he does not do so from faith, and whatever is not from faith is sin.

CHAPTER 15

EXHORTATION FOR THE STRONG TO HELP THE WEAK

But we who are strong ought to bear with the failings of the weak, and not just please ourselves. Let each of us please his neighbor for his good to build him up. For even Christ did not please himself, but just as it is written, *"The insults of those who insult you have fallen on me."* For everything that was written in former times was written for our instruction, so that through endurance and through encouragement of the scriptures we may have hope. Now may the God of endurance and comfort give you unity with one another in accordance with Christ Jesus, so that together you may with one voice glorify the God and Father of our Lord Jesus Christ.

EXHORTATION TO MUTUAL ACCEPTANCE

Receive one another, then, just as Christ also received you, to God's glory. For I tell you that Christ has become a servant of the circumcised on behalf of God's truth to confirm the promises made to the fathers, and thus the Gentiles glorify God for his mercy. As it is written, *"Because of this I will confess you among the Gentiles, and I will sing praises to your name."* And again it says: *"Rejoice, O Gentiles, with his people."* And again, *"Praise the Lord all you Gentiles, and let all the peoples praise him."* And again Isaiah says, *"The root of Jesse will come, and the one who rises to rule over the Gentiles, in him will the Gentiles hope."* Now may the God of hope fill you with all joy and peace as you believe in him, so that you may abound in hope by the power of the Holy Spirit.

PAUL'S MOTIVATION FOR WRITING THE LETTER

But I myself am fully convinced about you, my brothers and sisters, that you yourselves are full of goodness, filled with all knowledge, and able to instruct one another. But I have written more boldly to you on some points so as to remind you, because of the grace given to me by God to be a minister of Christ Jesus to the Gentiles. I serve the gospel of God like a priest, so that the Gentiles may become an acceptable offering, sanctified by the Holy Spirit.

So I boast in Christ Jesus about the things that pertain to God. For I will not dare to speak of anything except what Christ has accomplished through me in order to bring about the obedience of the Gentiles, by word and deed, in the power of signs and wonders, in the power of the Spirit of God. So from Jerusalem even as far as Illyricum I have fully preached the gospel of Christ. And in this way I desire to preach where Christ has not been named, so as not to build on another person's foundation, but as it is written: *"Those who were not told about him will see, and those who have not heard will understand."*

PAUL'S INTENTION OF VISITING THE ROMANS

This is the reason I was often hindered from coming to you. But now there is nothing more to keep me in these regions, and I have for many years desired to come to you when I go to Spain. For I hope to visit you when I pass through and that you will help me on my journey there, after I have enjoyed your company for a while.

But now I go to Jerusalem to minister to the saints. For Macedonia and Achaia are pleased to make some contribution for the poor among the saints in Jerusalem. For they were pleased to do this, and indeed they are indebted to the Jerusalem saints. For if the Gentiles have shared in their spiritual things, they are obligated also to minister to them in material things. Therefore after I have completed this and have safely delivered this bounty to them, I will set out for Spain by way of you, and I know that when I come to you, I will come in the fullness of Christ's blessing.

Now I urge you, brothers and sisters, through our Lord Jesus Christ and through the love of the Spirit, to join fervently with me in prayer to God on my behalf. Pray that I may be rescued from those who are disobedient in Judea and that my ministry in Jerusalem may be acceptable to the saints, so that by God's will I may come to you with joy and be refreshed in your company. Now may the God of peace be with all of you. Amen.

CHAPTER 16

PERSONAL GREETINGS

Now I commend to you our sister Phoebe, who is a servant of the church in Cenchrea, so that you may welcome her in the Lord in a way worthy of the saints and provide her with whatever help she may need from you, for she has been a great help to many, including me.

Greet Prisca and Aquila, my fellow workers in Christ Jesus, who risked their own necks for my life. Not only I, but all the churches of the Gentiles are grateful to them. Also greet the church in their house. Greet my dear friend Epenetus, who was the first convert to Christ in the province of Asia. Greet Mary, who has worked very hard for you. Greet Andronicus and Junia, my compatriots and my fellow prisoners. They are well known to the apostles, and they were in Christ before me. Greet Ampliatus, my dear friend in the Lord. Greet Urbanus, our fellow worker in Christ, and my good friend Stachys. Greet Apelles, who is approved in Christ. Greet those who belong to the household of Aristobulus. Greet Herodion, my compatriot. Greet those in the household of Narcissus who are in the Lord. Greet Tryphena and Tryphosa, laborers in the Lord. Greet my dear friend Persis, who has worked hard in the Lord. Greet Rufus, chosen in the Lord, and his mother who was also a mother to me. Greet Asyncritus, Phlegon, Hermes, Patrobas, Hermas, and the brothers and sisters with them. Greet Philologus and Julia, Nereus and his sister, and Olympas, and all the believers who are with them. Greet one another with a holy kiss. All the churches of Christ greet you.

Now I urge you, brothers and sisters, to watch out for those who create dissensions and obstacles contrary to the teaching that you learned. Avoid them! For these are the kind who do not serve our Lord Christ, but their own appetites. By their smooth talk and flattery they deceive the minds of the naive. Your obedience is known to all and thus I rejoice over you. But I want you to be wise in what is good and innocent in what is evil. The God of peace will quickly crush Satan under your feet. The grace of our Lord Jesus be with you.

Timothy, my fellow worker, greets you; so do Lucius, Jason, and Sosipater, my compatriots. I, Tertius, who am writing this letter, greet you in the Lord. Gaius, who is host to me and to the whole church, greets you. Erastus the city treasurer and our brother Quartus greet you.

Now to him who is able to strengthen you according to my gospel and the proclamation of Jesus Christ, according to the revelation of the mystery that had been kept secret for long ages, but now is disclosed, and through the prophetic scriptures has been made known to all the nations, according to the command of the eternal God, to bring about the obedience of faith—to the only wise God, through Jesus Christ, be glory forever! Amen.

1 CORINTHIANS

PROLOGUE

After planting the church in Corinth, Paul stayed in the city for about 18 months to help the church find its footing. The apostle had long left Corinth when men from that city arrived to tell him about several troubling developments. The church was struggling and needed his help.

The concerns were serious enough to warrant a visit. Paul loved the Corinthian church and he wanted to go, but he was in Ephesus in the middle of his third missionary journey. He could not leave this important work. But he could provide help through a letter. Paul wrote to the church, addressing each issue: division, immorality, litigation, marriage, idolatry, abuse of gifts, and denial of resurrection. The issues might seem disconnected, but Paul recognized the thread that ran through them all. He also knew the solution. If the people listened, they could deal with these problems and avoid others. The Corinthians were probably tempted to blame their sinful city for their problems, but the source was much closer. They would have to look within. And they would have to do that together.

CHAPTER 1

SALUTATION

From Paul, called to be an apostle of Christ Jesus by the will of God, and Sosthenes, our brother, to the church of God that is in Corinth, to those who are sanctified in Christ Jesus, and called to be saints, with all those in every place who call on the name of our Lord Jesus Christ, their Lord and ours. Grace and peace to you from God our Father and the Lord Jesus Christ!

THANKSGIVING

I always thank my God for you because of the grace of God that was given to you in Christ Jesus. For you were made rich in every way in him, in all your speech and in every kind of knowledge—just as the testimony about Christ has been confirmed among you—so that you do not lack any spiritual gift as you wait for the revelation of our Lord Jesus Christ. He will also strengthen you to the end, so that you will be blameless on the day of our Lord Jesus Christ. God is faithful, by whom you were called into fellowship with his son, Jesus Christ our Lord.

DIVISIONS IN THE CHURCH

I urge you, brothers and sisters, by the name of our Lord Jesus Christ, to agree together, to end your divisions, and to be united by the same mind and purpose. For members of

Chloe's household have made it clear to me, my brothers and sisters, that there are quarrels among you. Now I mean this, that each of you is saying, "I am with Paul," or "I am with Apollos," or "I am with Cephas," or "I am with Christ." Is Christ divided? Paul wasn't crucified for you, was he? Or were you in fact baptized in the name of Paul? I thank God that I did not baptize any of you except Crispus and Gaius, so that no one can say that you were baptized in my name! (I also baptized the household of Stephanus. Otherwise, I do not remember whether I baptized anyone else.) For Christ did not send me to baptize, but to preach the gospel—and not with clever speech, so that the cross of Christ would not become useless.

THE MESSAGE OF THE CROSS

For the message about the cross is foolishness to those who are perishing, but to us who are being saved it is the power of God. For it is written, *"I will destroy the wisdom of the wise, and I will thwart the cleverness of the intelligent."* Where is the wise man? Where is the expert in the Mosaic law? Where is the debater of this age? Has God not made the wisdom of the world foolish? For since in the wisdom of God the world by its wisdom did not know God, God was pleased to save those who believe by the foolishness of preaching. For Jews demand miraculous signs and

Greeks ask for wisdom, but we preach about a crucified Christ, a stumbling block to Jews and foolishness to Gentiles. But to those who are called, both Jews and Greeks, Christ is the power of God and the wisdom of God. For the foolishness of God is wiser than human wisdom, and the weakness of God is stronger than human strength.

Think about the circumstances of your call, brothers and sisters. Not many were wise by human standards, not many were powerful, not many were born to a privileged position. But God chose what the world thinks foolish to shame the wise, and God chose what the world thinks weak to shame the strong. God chose what is low and despised in the world, what is regarded as nothing, to set aside what is regarded as something, so that no one can boast in his presence. He is the reason you have a relationship with Christ Jesus, who became for us wisdom from God, and righteousness and sanctification and redemption, so that, as it is written, *"Let the one who boasts, boast in the Lord."*

CHAPTER 2

When I came to you, brothers and sisters, I did not come with superior eloquence or wisdom as I proclaimed the testimony of God. For I decided to be concerned about nothing among you except Jesus Christ, and him crucified. And I was with you in weakness and in fear and with much trembling. My conversation and my preaching were not with persuasive words of wisdom, but with a demonstration of the Spirit and of power, so that your faith would not be based on human wisdom but on the power of God.

WISDOM FROM GOD

Now we do speak wisdom among the mature, but not a wisdom of this age or of the rulers of this age, who are perishing. Instead we speak the wisdom of God, hidden in a mystery, that God determined before the ages for our glory. None of the rulers of this age understood it. If they had known it, they would not have crucified the Lord of glory. But just as it is written, *"Things that no eye has seen, or ear heard, or mind imagined, are the things God has prepared for those who love him."* God has revealed these to us by the Spirit. For the Spirit searches all things, even the deep things of God. For who among men knows the things of a man except the man's spirit within him? So too, no one knows the things of God except the Spirit of God. Now we have not received the spirit of the world, but the Spirit who is from God, so that we may know the things that are freely given to us by God. And we speak about these things, not with words taught us by human wisdom, but with those taught by the Spirit, explaining spiritual things to spiritual people. The unbeliever does not receive the things of the Spirit of God, for they are foolishness to him. And he cannot understand them, because they are spiritually discerned. The one who is spiritual discerns all things, yet he himself is understood by no one. *For who has known the mind of the Lord, so as to advise him?* But we have the mind of Christ.

CHAPTER 3

IMMATURITY AND SELF-DECEPTION

So, brothers and sisters, I could not speak to you as spiritual people, but instead as people of the flesh, as infants in Christ. I fed you milk, not solid food, for you were not yet ready. In fact, you are still not ready, for you are still influenced by the flesh. For since there is still jealousy and dissension among you, are you not influenced by the flesh and behaving like unregenerate people? For whenever someone says, "I am with Paul," or "I am with Apollos," are you not merely human?

What is Apollos, really? Or what is Paul? Servants through whom you came to believe, and each of us in the ministry the Lord gave us. I planted, Apollos watered, but God caused it to grow. So neither the one who plants counts for anything, nor the one who waters, but God who causes the growth. The one who plants and the one who waters work as one, but each will receive his reward according to his work. We are coworkers belonging to God. You are God's field, God's building. According to the grace of God given to me, like a skilled master-builder I laid a foundation, but someone else builds on it. And each one must be careful how he builds. For no one can lay any foundation other than what is being laid, which is Jesus Christ. If anyone builds on the foundation with gold, silver, precious stones, wood, hay, or straw, each builder's work will be plainly seen, for the Day will make it clear, because it will be revealed by fire. And the fire will test what kind of work each has done. If what someone has built survives, he will receive a reward. If someone's work is burned up, he will suffer loss. He himself will be saved, but only as through fire.

Do you not know that you are God's temple and that God's Spirit lives in you? If someone destroys God's temple, God will destroy him. For God's temple is holy, which is what you are.

Guard against self-deception, each of you. If someone among you thinks he is wise in this age, let him become foolish so that he can become wise. For the wisdom of this age is foolishness with God. As it is written, *"He catches the wise in their craftiness."* And again, *"The Lord knows that the thoughts of the wise are futile."* So then, no more boasting about mere mortals! For everything belongs to you, whether Paul or Apollos or Cephas or the world or life or death or the present or the future. Everything belongs to you, and you belong to Christ, and Christ belongs to God.

CHAPTER 4

THE APOSTLES' MINISTRY

One should think about us this way—as servants of Christ and stewards of the mysteries of God. Now what is sought in stewards is that one be found faithful. So for me, it is a minor matter that I am judged by you or by any human court. In fact, I do not even judge myself. For I am not aware of anything against myself, but I am not acquitted because of this. The one who judges me is the Lord. So then, do not judge anything before the time. Wait until the Lord comes. He will bring to light the hidden things of darkness and reveal the motives of hearts. Then each will receive recognition from God.

I have applied these things to myself and Apollos because of you, brothers and sisters, so that through us you may learn "not to go beyond what is written," so that none of you will be puffed up in favor of the one against the other. For who concedes you any superiority? What do you have that you did not receive? And if you received it, why do you boast as though you did not? Already you are satisfied! Already you are rich! You have become kings without us! I wish you had become kings so that we could reign with you! For, I think, God has exhibited us apostles last of all, as men condemned to die, because we have become a spectacle to the world, both to angels and to people. We are fools for Christ, but you are wise in Christ! We are weak, but you are strong! You are distinguished, we are dishonored! To the present hour we are hungry and thirsty, poorly clothed, brutally treated, and without a roof over our heads. We do hard work, toiling with our own hands. When we are verbally abused, we respond with a blessing, when persecuted, we endure, when people lie about us, we answer in a friendly manner. We are the world's dirt and scum, even now.

A FATHER'S WARNING

I am not writing these things to shame you, but to correct you as my dear children. For though you may have 10,000 guardians in Christ, you do not have many fathers, because I became your father in Christ Jesus through the gospel. I encourage you, then, be imitators of me. For this reason, I have sent Timothy to you, who is my dear and faithful son in the Lord. He will remind you of my ways in Christ, as I teach them everywhere in every church. Some have become arrogant, as if I were not coming to you. But I will come to you soon, if the Lord is willing, and I will find out not only the talk of these arrogant people, but also their power. For the kingdom of God is demonstrated not in idle talk but with power. What do you want? Shall I come to you with a rod of discipline or with love and a spirit of gentleness?

CHAPTER 5

CHURCH DISCIPLINE

It is actually reported that sexual immorality exists among you, the kind of immorality that is not permitted even among the Gentiles, so that someone is cohabiting with his father's wife. And you are proud! Shouldn't you have been deeply sorrowful instead and removed the one who did this from among you? For even though I am absent physically, I am present in spirit. And I have already judged the one who did this, just as though I were present. When you gather together in the name of our Lord Jesus, and I am with you in spirit, along with the power of our Lord Jesus, hand this man over to Satan for the destruction of the flesh, so that his spirit may be saved in the day of the Lord.

Your boasting is not good. Don't you know that a little yeast affects the whole batch of dough? Clean out the old yeast so that you may be a new batch of dough—you are, in fact, without yeast. For Christ, our Passover lamb, has been sacrificed. So then, let us celebrate the festival, not with the old yeast, the yeast of vice and evil, but with the bread without yeast, the bread of sincerity and truth.

I wrote you in my letter not to associate with sexually immoral people. In no way did I mean the immoral people of this world, or the greedy and swindlers and idolaters, since you would then have to go out of the world. But now I am writing to you not to associate with anyone who calls himself a Christian who is sexually immoral, or greedy, or an idolater, or verbally abusive, or a drunkard, or a swindler. Do not even eat with such a person. For what do I have to do with judging those outside? Are you not to judge those inside? But God will judge those outside. *Remove the evil person from among you.*

CHAPTER 6

LAWSUITS

When any of you has a legal dispute with another, does he dare go to court before the unrighteous rather than before the saints? Or do you not know that the saints will judge the world? And if the world is to be judged by you, are you not competent to settle trivial suits? Do you not know that we will judge angels? Why not ordinary matters! So if you have ordinary lawsuits, do you appoint as judges those who have no standing in the church? I say this to your shame! Is there no one among you wise enough to settle disputes between fellow Christians? Instead, does a Christian sue a Christian, and do this before unbelievers? The fact that you have lawsuits among yourselves demonstrates that you have already been defeated. Why not rather be wronged? Why not rather be cheated? But you yourselves wrong and cheat, and you do this to your brothers and sisters!

Do you not know that the unrighteous will not inherit the kingdom of God? Do not be deceived! The sexually immoral, idolaters, adulterers, passive homosexual partners, practicing homosexuals, thieves, the greedy, drunkards, the verbally abusive, and swindlers will not inherit the kingdom of God. Some of you once lived this way. But you were washed, you were sanctified, you were justified in the name of the Lord Jesus Christ and by the Spirit of our God.

FLEE SEXUAL IMMORALITY

"All things are lawful for me"—but not everything is beneficial. "All things are lawful for me"—but I will not be controlled by anything. "Food is for the stomach and the stomach is for food, but God will do away with both." The body is not for sexual immorality, but for the Lord, and the Lord for the body. Now God indeed raised the Lord and he will raise us by his power. Do you not know that your bodies are members of Christ? Should I take the members of Christ and make them members of a prostitute? Never! Or do you not know that anyone who is united with a prostitute is one body with her? For it is said, *"The two will become one flesh."* But the one united with the Lord is one spirit with him. Flee sexual immorality! "Every sin a person commits is outside of the body"—but the immoral person sins against his own body. Or do you not know that your body is the temple of the Holy Spirit who is in you, whom you have from God, and you are not your own? For you were bought at a price. Therefore glorify God with your body.

CHAPTER 7

CELIBACY AND MARRIAGE

Now with regard to the issues you wrote about: "It is good for a man not to have sexual relations with a woman." But because of immoralities, each man should have relations with his own wife and each woman with her own husband. A husband should fulfill his marital responsibility to his wife, and likewise a wife to her husband. It is not the wife who has the rights to her own body, but the husband. In the same way, it is not the husband who has the rights to his own body, but the wife. Do not deprive each other, except by mutual agreement for a specified time, so that you may devote yourselves to prayer. Then resume your relationship, so that Satan may not tempt you because of your lack of self-control. I say this as a concession, not as a command. I wish that everyone was as I am. But each has his own gift from God, one this way, another that.

To the unmarried and widows I say that it is best for them to remain as I am. But if they do not have self-control, let them get married. For it is better to marry than to burn with sexual desire.

To the married I give this command—not I, but the Lord—a wife should not divorce a husband (but if she does, let her remain unmarried, or be reconciled to her husband), and a husband should not divorce his wife.

To the rest I say—I, not the Lord—if a brother has a wife who is not a believer and she is happy to live with him, he should not divorce her. And if a woman has a husband who is not a believer and he is happy to live with her, she should not divorce him. For the unbelieving husband is sanctified because of the wife, and the unbelieving wife because of her husband. Otherwise your children are unclean, but now they are holy. But if the unbeliever wants a divorce, let it take place. In these circumstances the brother or sister is not bound. God has called you in peace. For how do you know, wife, whether you will bring your husband to salvation? Or how do you know, husband, whether you will bring your wife to salvation?

THE CIRCUMSTANCES OF YOUR CALLING

Nevertheless, as the Lord has assigned to each one, as God has called each person, so must he live. I give this sort of direction in all the churches. Was anyone called after he had been circumcised? He should not try to undo his circumcision. Was anyone called who is uncircumcised? He should not get circumcised. Circumcision is nothing and uncircumcision is nothing. Instead, keeping God's commandments is what counts. Let each one remain in that situation in life in which he was called. Were you called as a slave? Do not worry about it. But if indeed you are able to be free, make the most of the opportunity. For the one who was called in the Lord as a slave is the Lord's freedman. In the same way, the one who was called as a free person is Christ's slave. You were bought with a price. Do not become slaves of men. In whatever situation someone was called, brothers and sisters, let him remain in it with God.

REMAINING UNMARRIED

With regard to the question about people who have never married, I have no command from the Lord, but I give my opinion as one shown mercy by the Lord to be trustworthy. Because of the impending crisis I think it best for you to remain as you are. The one bound to a wife should not seek divorce. The one released from a wife should not seek marriage. But if you marry, you have not sinned. And if a virgin marries, she has not sinned. But those who marry will face difficult circumstances, and I am trying to spare you such problems. And I say this, brothers and sisters: The time is short. So then those who have wives should be as those who have none, those with tears like those not weeping, those who rejoice like those not rejoicing, those who buy like those without possessions, those who use the world as though they were not using it to the full. For the present shape of this world is passing away.

And I want you to be free from concern. An unmarried man is concerned about the things of the Lord, how to please the Lord. But a married man is concerned about the things of the world, how to please his wife, and he is divided. An unmarried woman or a virgin is concerned about the things of the Lord, to be holy both in body and spirit. But a married woman is concerned about the things of the world, how to please her husband. I am saying this for your benefit, not to place a limitation on you, but so that without distraction you may give notable and constant service to the Lord.

If anyone thinks he is acting inappropriately toward his virgin, if she is past the bloom of youth and it seems necessary, he should do what he wishes; he does not sin. Let them marry. But the man who is firm in his commitment, and is under no necessity but has control over his will, and has decided in his own mind to keep his own virgin, does well. So then, the one who marries his own virgin does well, but the one who does not, does better.

A wife is bound as long as her husband is living. But if her husband dies, she is free to marry anyone she wishes (only someone in the Lord). But in my opinion, she will be happier if she remains as she is—and I think that I too have the Spirit of God!

CHAPTER 8

FOOD SACRIFICED TO IDOLS

With regard to food sacrificed to idols, we know that "we all have knowledge." Knowledge puffs up, but love builds up. If someone thinks he knows something, he does not yet know to the degree that he needs to know. But if someone loves God, he is known by God.

With regard then to eating food sacrificed to idols, we know that "an idol in this world is nothing," and that "there is no God but one." If after all there are so-called gods, whether in heaven or on earth (as there are many gods and many lords), yet for us there is one God, the Father, from whom are all things and for whom we live, and one Lord, Jesus Christ, through whom are all things and through whom we live.

But this knowledge is not shared by all. And some, by being accustomed to idols in former times, eat this food as an idol sacrifice, and their conscience, because it is weak, is defiled. Now food will not bring us close to God. We are no worse if we do not eat and no better if we do. But be careful that this liberty of yours does not become a hindrance to the weak. For if someone weak sees you who possess knowledge dining in an idol's temple, will not his conscience be "strengthened" to eat food offered to idols? So by your knowledge the weak brother or sister, for whom Christ died, is destroyed. If you sin against your brothers or sisters in this way and wound their weak conscience, you sin against Christ. For this reason, if food causes my brother or sister to sin, I will never eat meat again, so that I may not cause one of them to sin.

CHAPTER 9

THE RIGHTS OF AN APOSTLE

Am I not free? Am I not an apostle? Have I not seen Jesus our Lord? Are you not my work in the Lord? If I am not an apostle to others, at least I am to you, for you are the confirming sign of my apostleship in the Lord. This is my defense to those who examine me. Do we not have the right to financial support? Do we not have the right to the company of a believing wife, like the other apostles and the Lord's brothers and Cephas? Or do only Barnabas and I lack the right not to work? Who ever serves in the army at his own expense? Who plants a vineyard and does not eat its fruit? Who tends a flock and does not consume its milk? Am I saying these things only on the basis of common sense, or does the law not say this as well? For it is written in the law of Moses, **"Do not muzzle an ox while it is treading out the grain."** God is not concerned here about oxen, is he? Or is he not surely speaking for our benefit? It was written for us, because the one plowing and threshing ought to work in hope of enjoying the harvest. If we sowed spiritual blessings among you, is it too much to reap material things from you? If others receive this right from you, are we not more deserving?

But we have not made use of this right. Instead we endure everything so that we may not be a hindrance to the gospel of Christ. Don't you know that those who serve in the temple eat food from the temple, and those who serve at the altar receive a part of the offerings? In the same way the Lord commanded those who proclaim the gospel to receive their living by the gospel. But I have not used any of these rights. And I am not writing these things so that something will be done for me. In fact, it would be better for me to die than—no one will deprive me of my reason for boasting! For if I preach the gospel, I have no reason for boasting, because I am compelled to do this. Woe to me if I do not preach the gospel! For if I do this voluntarily, I have a reward. But if I do it unwillingly, I am entrusted with a responsibility. What then is my reward? That when I preach the gospel I may offer the gospel free of charge, and so not make full use of my rights in the gospel.

For since I am free from all I can make myself a slave to all, in order to gain even more people. To the Jews I became like a Jew to gain the Jews. To those under the law I became like one under the law (though I myself am not under the law) to gain those under the law. To those free from the law I became like one free from the law (though I am not free from God's law but under the law of Christ) to gain those free from the law. To the weak I became weak in order to gain the weak. I have become all things to all people, so that by all means I may save some.

I do all these things because of the gospel, so that I can be a participant in it.

Do you not know that all the runners in a stadium compete, but only one receives the prize? So run to win. Each competitor must exercise self-control in everything. They do it to receive a perishable crown, but we an imperishable one.

So I do not run uncertainly or box like one who hits only air. Instead I subdue my body and make it my slave, so that after preaching to others I myself will not be disqualified.

CHAPTER 10

LEARNING FROM ISRAEL'S FAILURES

For I do not want you to be unaware, brothers and sisters, that our fathers were all under the cloud and all passed through the sea, and all were baptized into Moses in the cloud and in the sea, and all ate the same spiritual food, and all drank the same spiritual drink. For they were all drinking from the spiritual rock that followed them, and the rock was Christ. But God was not pleased with most of them, for they were cut down in the wilderness. These things happened as examples for us, so that we will not crave evil things as they did. So do not be idolaters, as some of them were. As it is written, ***"The people sat down to eat and drink and rose up to play."*** And let us not be immoral, as some of them were, and 23,000 died in a single day. And let us not put Christ to the test, as some of them did, and were destroyed by snakes. And do not complain, as some of them did, and were killed by the destroying angel. These things happened to them as examples and were written for our instruction, on whom the ends of the ages have come. So let the one who thinks he is standing be careful that he does not fall. No trial has overtaken you that is not faced by others. And God is faithful: He will not let you be tried beyond what you are able to bear, but with the trial will also provide a way out so that you may be able to endure it.

AVOID IDOL FEASTS

So then, my dear friends, flee from idolatry. I am speaking to thoughtful people. Consider what I say. Is not the cup of blessing that we bless a sharing in the blood of Christ? Is not the bread that we break a sharing in the body of Christ? Because there is one bread, we who are many are one body, for we all share the one bread. Look at the people of Israel. Are not those who eat the sacrifices partners in the altar? Am I saying that idols or food sacrificed to them amount to anything? No, I mean that what the pagans sacrifice is to demons and not to God. I do not want you to be partners with demons. You cannot drink the cup of the Lord and the cup of demons. You cannot take part in the table of the Lord and the table of demons. Or are we trying to provoke the Lord to jealousy? Are we really stronger than he is?

LIVE TO GLORIFY GOD

"Everything is lawful," but not everything is beneficial. "Everything is lawful," but not everything builds others up. Do not seek your own good, but the good of the other person. Eat anything that is sold in the marketplace without questions of conscience, for *the earth and its abundance are the Lord's*. If an unbeliever invites you to dinner and you want to go, eat whatever is served without asking questions of conscience. But if someone says to you, "This is from a sacrifice," do not eat, because of the one who told you and because of conscience—I do not mean yours but the other person's. For why is my freedom being judged by another's conscience? If I partake with thankfulness, why am I blamed for the food that I give thanks for? So whether you eat or drink, or whatever you do, do everything for the glory of God. Do not give offense to Jews or Greeks or to the church of God, just as I also try to please everyone in all things. I do not seek my own benefit, but the benefit of many, so that they may be saved.

CHAPTER 11

Be imitators of me, just as I also am of Christ.

WOMEN'S HEAD COVERINGS

I praise you because you remember me in everything and maintain the traditions just as I passed them on to you. But I want you to know that Christ is the head of every man, and the man is the head of a woman, and God is the head of Christ. Any man who prays or prophesies with his head covered disgraces his head. But any woman who prays or prophesies with her head uncovered disgraces her head, for it is one and the same thing as having a shaved head. For if a woman will not cover her head, she should cut off her hair. But if it is disgraceful for a woman to have her hair cut off or her head shaved, she should cover her head. For a man should not have his head covered, since he is the image and glory of God. But the woman is the glory of the man. For man did not come from woman, but woman from man. Neither was man created for the sake of woman, but woman for man. For this reason a woman should have a symbol of authority on her head, because of the angels. In any case, in the Lord woman is not independent of man, nor is man independent of woman. For just as woman came from man, so man comes through woman. But all things come from God. Judge for yourselves: Is it proper for a woman to pray to God with her head uncovered? Does not nature itself teach you that if a man has long hair, it is a disgrace for him, but if a woman has long hair, it is her glory? For her hair is given to her for a covering. If anyone intends to quarrel about this, we have no other practice, nor do the churches of God.

THE LORD'S SUPPER

Now in giving the following instruction I do not praise you, because you come together not for the better but for the worse. For in the first place, when you come together as a church I hear there are divisions among you, and in part I believe it. For there must in fact be divisions among you, so that those of you who are approved may be evident. Now when you come together at the same place, you are not really eating the Lord's Supper. For when it is time to eat, everyone proceeds with his own supper. One is hungry and another becomes drunk. Do you not have houses so that you can eat and drink? Or are you trying to show contempt for the church of God by shaming those who have nothing? What should I say to you? Should I praise you? I will not praise you for this!

For I received from the Lord what I also passed on to you, that the Lord Jesus on the night in which he was betrayed took bread, and after he had given thanks he broke it and said, "This is my body, which is for you. Do this in remembrance of me." In the same way, he also took the cup after supper, saying, "This cup is the new covenant in my blood. Do this, every time you drink it, in remembrance of me." For every time you eat this bread and drink the cup, you proclaim the Lord's death until he comes.

For this reason, whoever eats the bread or drinks the cup of the Lord in an unworthy manner will be guilty of the body and blood of the Lord. A person should examine himself first, and in this way let him eat the bread and drink of the cup. For the one who eats and drinks without careful regard for the body eats and drinks judgment against himself. That is why many of you are weak and sick, and quite a few are dead. But if we examined ourselves, we would not be judged. But when we are judged by the Lord, we are disciplined so that we may not be condemned with the world. So then, my brothers and sisters, when you come together to eat, wait for one another. If anyone is hungry, let him eat at home, so that when you assemble it does not lead to judgment. I will give directions about other matters when I come.

CHAPTER 12

SPIRITUAL GIFTS

With regard to spiritual gifts, brothers and sisters, I do not want you to be uninformed. You know that when you were pagans you were often led astray by speechless idols, however you were led. So I want you to understand that no one speaking by the Spirit of God says, "Jesus is cursed," and no one can say, "Jesus is Lord," except by the Holy Spirit.

Now there are different gifts, but the same Spirit. And there are different ministries, but the same Lord. And there are different results, but the same God who produces all of them in everyone. To each person the manifestation of the Spirit is given for the benefit of all. For one person is given through the Spirit the message of wisdom, and another the message of knowledge according to the same Spirit, to another faith by the same Spirit, and to another gifts of healing by the one Spirit, to another performance of miracles, to another prophecy, and to another discernment of spirits, to another different kinds of tongues, and to another the interpretation of tongues. It is one and the same Spirit, distributing as he decides to each person, who produces all these things.

DIFFERENT MEMBERS IN ONE BODY

For just as the body is one and yet has many members, and all the members of the body—though many—are one body, so too is Christ. For in one Spirit we were all baptized into one body. Whether Jews or Greeks or slaves or free, we were all made to drink of the one Spirit. For in fact the body is not a single member, but many. If the foot says, "Since I am not a hand, I am not part of the body," it does not lose its membership in the body because of that. And if the ear says, "Since I am not an eye, I am not part of the body," it does not lose its membership in the body because of that. If the whole body were an eye, what part would do the hearing? If the whole were an ear, what part would exercise the sense of smell? But as a matter of fact, God has placed each of the members in the body just as he decided. If they were all the same member, where would the body be? So now there are many members, but one body. The eye cannot say to the hand, "I do not need you," nor in turn can the head say to the foot, "I do not need you." On the contrary, those members that seem to be weaker are essential, and those members we consider less honorable we clothe with greater honor, and our unpresentable members are clothed with dignity, but our presentable members do not need this. Instead, God has blended together the body, giving greater honor to the lesser member, so that there may be no division in the body, but the members may have mutual concern for one another. If one member suffers, everyone suffers with it. If a member is honored, all rejoice with it.

Now you are Christ's body, and each of you is a member of it. And God has placed in the church first apostles, second prophets, third teachers, then miracles, gifts of healing, helps, gifts of leadership, different kinds of tongues. Not all are apostles, are they? Not all are prophets, are they? Not all are teachers, are they? Not all perform miracles, do they? Not all have gifts of healing, do they? Not all speak in tongues, do they? Not all interpret, do they? But you should be eager for the greater gifts.

And now I will show you a way that is beyond comparison.

CHAPTER 13

THE WAY OF LOVE

If I speak in the tongues of men and of angels, but I do not have love, I am a noisy gong or a clanging cymbal. And if I have prophecy, and know all mysteries and all knowledge, and if I have all faith so that I can remove mountains, but do not have love, I am nothing. If I give away everything I own, and if I give over my body in order to boast, but do not have love, I receive no benefit.

Love is patient, love is kind, it is not envious.

Love does not brag, it is not puffed up. It is not rude, it is not self-serving, it is not easily angered or resentful. It is not glad about injustice, but rejoices in the truth. It bears all things, believes all things, hopes all things, endures all things.

Love never ends. But if there are prophecies, they will be set aside; if there are tongues, they will cease; if there is knowledge, it will be set aside. For we know in part, and we prophesy in part, but when what is perfect comes, the partial will be set aside. When I was a child, I talked like a child, I thought like a child, I reasoned like a child. But when I became an adult, I set aside childish ways. For now we see in a mirror indirectly, but then we will see face to face. Now I know in part, but then I will know fully, just as I have been fully known. And now these three remain: faith, hope, and love. But the greatest of these is love.

CHAPTER 14

PROPHECY AND TONGUES

Pursue love and be eager for the spiritual gifts, especially that you may prophesy. For the one speaking in a tongue does not speak to people but to God, for no one understands; he is speaking mysteries by the Spirit. But the one who prophesies speaks to people for their strengthening, encouragement, and consolation. The one who speaks in a tongue builds himself up, but the one who prophesies builds up the church. I wish you all spoke in tongues, but even more that you would prophesy. The one who prophesies is greater than the one who speaks in tongues, unless he interprets so that the church may be strengthened.

Now, brothers and sisters, if I come to you speaking in tongues, how will I help you unless I speak to you with a revelation or with knowledge or prophecy or teaching? It is similar for lifeless things that make a sound, like a flute or harp. Unless they make a distinction in the notes, how can what is played on the flute or harp be understood? If, for example, the trumpet makes an unclear sound, who will get ready for battle? It is the same for you. If you do not speak clearly with your tongue, how will anyone know what is being said? For you will be speaking into the air. There are probably many kinds of languages in the world, and none is without meaning. If then I do not know the meaning of a language, I will be a foreigner to the speaker and the speaker a foreigner to me. It is the same with you. Since you are eager for manifestations of the Spirit, seek to abound in order to strengthen the church.

So then, one who speaks in a tongue should pray that he may interpret. If I pray in a tongue, my spirit prays, but my mind is unproductive. What should I do? I will pray with my spirit, but I will also pray with my mind. I will sing praises with my spirit, but I will also sing praises with my mind. Otherwise, if you are praising God with your spirit, how can someone without the gift say "Amen" to your thanksgiving, since he does not know what you are saying? For you are certainly giving thanks well, but the other person is not strengthened. I thank God that I speak in tongues more than all of you, but in the church I want to speak five words with my mind to instruct others, rather than ten thousand words in a tongue.

Brothers and sisters, do not be children in your thinking. Instead, be infants in evil, but in your thinking be mature. It is written in the law: *"By people with strange tongues and by the lips of strangers I will speak to this people, yet not even in this way will they listen to me,"* says the Lord. So then, tongues are a sign not for believers but for unbelievers. Prophecy, however, is not for unbelievers but for believers. So if the whole church comes together and all speak in tongues, and unbelievers or uninformed people enter, will they not say that you have lost your minds? But if all prophesy, and an unbeliever or uninformed person enters, he will be convicted by all, he will be called to account by all. The secrets of his heart are disclosed, and in this way he will fall down with his face to the ground and worship God, declaring, "God is really among you."

CHURCH ORDER

What should you do then, brothers and sisters? When you come together, each one has a song, has a lesson, has a revelation, has a tongue, has an interpretation. Let all these things be done for the strengthening of the church. If someone speaks in a tongue, it should be two, or at the most three, one after the other, and someone must interpret. But if there is no interpreter, he should be silent in the church. Let him speak to himself and to God. Two or three prophets should speak and the others should evaluate what is said. And if someone sitting down receives a revelation, the person who is speaking should conclude. For you can all prophesy one after another, so all can learn and be encouraged. Indeed, the spirits of the prophets are subject to the prophets, for God is not characterized by disorder but by peace.

As in all the churches of the saints, the women should be silent in the churches, for they are not permitted to speak. Rather, let them be in submission, as in fact the law says. If they want to find out about something, they should ask their husbands at home, because it is disgraceful for a woman to speak in church. Did the word of God begin with you, or did it come to you alone?

If anyone considers himself a prophet or spiritual person, he should acknowledge that what I write to you is the Lord's command. If someone does not recognize this, he is not recognized. So then, brothers and sisters, be eager to prophesy, and do not forbid anyone from speaking in tongues. And do everything in a decent and orderly manner.

CHAPTER 15

CHRIST'S RESURRECTION

Now I want to make clear for you, brothers and sisters, the gospel that I preached to you, that you received and on which you stand, and by which you are being saved, if you hold firmly to the message I preached to you—unless you believed in vain. For I passed on to you as of first importance what I also received—that Christ died for our sins according to the scriptures, and that he was buried, and that he was raised on the third day according to the scriptures, and that he appeared to Cephas, then to the twelve. Then he appeared to more than 500 of the brothers and sisters at one time, most of whom are still alive, though some have fallen asleep. Then he appeared to James, then to all the apostles. Last of all, as though to one born at the wrong time, he appeared to me also. For I am the least of the apostles, unworthy to be called an apostle, because I persecuted the church of God. But by the grace of God I am what I am, and his grace to me has not been in vain. In fact, I worked harder than all of them—yet not I, but the grace of God with me. Whether then it was I or they, this is the way we preach and this is the way you believed.

NO RESURRECTION?

Now if Christ is being preached as raised from the dead, how can some of you say there is no resurrection of the dead? But if there is no resurrection of the dead, then not even Christ has been raised. And if Christ has not been raised, then our preaching is futile and your faith is empty. Also, we are found to be false witnesses about God, because we have testified against God that he raised Christ from the dead, when in reality he did not raise him, if indeed the dead are not raised. For if the dead are not raised, then not even Christ has been raised. And if Christ has not been raised, your faith is useless; you are still in your sins. Furthermore, those who have fallen asleep in Christ have also perished. For if only in this life we have hope in Christ, we should be pitied more than anyone.

But now Christ has been raised from the dead, the firstfruits of those who have fallen asleep. For since death came through a man, the resurrection of the dead also came through a man. For just as in Adam all die, so also in Christ all will be made alive. But each in his own order: Christ, the firstfruits; then when Christ comes, those who belong to him. Then comes the end, when he hands over the kingdom to God the Father, when he has brought to an end all rule and all authority and power. For he must reign until he has put all his enemies under his feet. The last enemy to be eliminated is death. For *he has put everything in subjection under his feet.* But when it says "everything" has been put in subjection, it is clear that this does not include the one who put everything in subjection to him. And when all things are subjected to him, then the Son himself will be subjected to the one who subjected everything to him, so that God may be all in all.

Otherwise, what will those do who are baptized for the dead? If the dead are not raised at all, then why are they baptized for them? Why too are we in danger every hour? Every day I am in danger of death! This is as sure as my boasting in you, which I have in Christ Jesus our Lord. If from a human point of view I fought with wild beasts at Ephesus, what did it benefit me? If the dead are not raised, *let us eat and drink, for tomorrow we die.* Do not be deceived: "Bad company corrupts good morals." Sober up as you should, and stop sinning! For some have no knowledge of God—I say this to your shame!

THE RESURRECTION BODY

But someone will say, "How are the dead raised? With what kind of body will they come?" Fool! What you sow will not come to life unless it dies. And what you sow is not the body that is to be, but a bare seed—perhaps of wheat or something else. But God gives it a body just as he planned, and to each of the seeds a body of its own. All flesh is not the same: People have one flesh, animals have another, birds and fish another. And there are heavenly bodies and earthly bodies. The glory of the heavenly body is one sort and the earthly another. There is one glory of the sun, and another glory of the moon and another glory of the stars, for star differs from star in glory.

It is the same with the resurrection of the dead. What is sown is perishable, what is raised is imperishable. It is sown in dishonor, it is raised in glory; it is sown in weakness, it is raised in power; it is sown a natural body, it is raised a spiritual body. If there is a natural body, there is also a spiritual body. So also it is written, *"The first man, Adam, became a living person"*; the last Adam became a life-giving spirit. However, the spiritual did not come first, but the natural, and then the spiritual. The first man is from the earth, made of dust; the second man is from heaven. Like the one made of dust, so too are those made of dust, and like the one from heaven, so too those who are heavenly. And just as we have borne the image of the man of dust, let us also bear the image of the man of heaven.

Now this is what I am saying, brothers and sisters: Flesh and blood cannot inherit the kingdom of God, nor does the perishable inherit the imperishable. Listen, I will tell you a mystery: We will not all sleep, but we will all be changed—in a moment, in the blinking of an eye, at the last trumpet. For the trumpet will sound, and the dead will be raised imperishable, and we will be changed. For this perishable body must put on the imperishable, and this mortal body must put on immortality. Now when this perishable puts on the imperishable, and this mortal puts on immortality, then the saying that is written will happen,

"Death has been swallowed up in victory."
"Where, O death, is your victory?
Where, O death, is your sting?"

The sting of death is sin, and the power of sin is the law. But thanks be to God, who gives us the victory through our Lord Jesus Christ! So then, dear brothers and sisters, be firm. Do not be moved! Always be outstanding in the work of the Lord, knowing that your labor is not in vain in the Lord.

CHAPTER 16

A COLLECTION TO AID JEWISH CHRISTIANS

With regard to the collection for the saints, please follow the directions that I gave to the churches of Galatia: On the first day of the week, each of you should set aside some income and save it to the extent that God has blessed you, so that a collection will not have to be made when I come. Then, when I arrive, I will send those whom you approve with letters of explanation to carry your gift to Jerusalem. And if it seems advisable that I should go also, they will go with me.

PAUL'S PLANS TO VISIT

But I will come to you after I have gone through Macedonia—for I will be going through Macedonia—and perhaps I will stay with you, or even spend the winter, so that you can send me on my journey, wherever I go. For I do not want to see you now in passing, since I hope to spend some time with you, if the Lord allows. But I will stay in Ephesus until Pentecost, because a door of great opportunity stands wide open for me, but there are many opponents.

Now if Timothy comes, see that he has nothing to fear among you, for he is doing the Lord's work, as I am too. So then, let no one treat him with contempt. But send him on his way in peace so that he may come to me. For I am expecting him with the brothers.

With regard to our brother Apollos: I strongly encouraged him to visit you with the other brothers, but it was simply not his intention to come now. He will come when he has the opportunity.

FINAL CHALLENGE AND BLESSING

Stay alert, stand firm in the faith, show courage, be strong. Everything you do should be done in love.

Now, brothers and sisters, you know about the household of Stephanus, that as the first converts of Achaia, they devoted themselves to ministry for the saints. I urge you also to submit to people like this, and to everyone who cooperates in the work and labors hard. I was glad about the arrival of Stephanus, Fortunatus, and Achaicus because they have supplied the fellowship with you that I lacked. For they refreshed my spirit and yours. So then, recognize people like this.

The churches in the province of Asia send greetings to you. Aquila and Prisca greet you warmly in the Lord, with the church that meets in their house. All the brothers and sisters send greetings. Greet one another with a holy kiss.

I, Paul, send this greeting with my own hand.

Let anyone who has no love for the Lord be accursed. Our Lord, come!

The grace of the Lord Jesus be with you.

My love be with all of you in Christ Jesus.

2 CORINTHIANS

PROLOGUE

Paul had sent a letter responding to the challenges the Corinthian church faced. Now Timothy brought a report on how the church had received Paul's letter. Unfortunately, intense opposition to the apostle had arisen in the church. Another letter would not do. It was time for Paul to go to Corinth and address the situation head-on.

His visit was painful and brief. Worse, it failed to resolve the issues. Afterward Paul sent another letter, a sorrowful one, to the church carried by Titus.

When Titus returned from Corinth, he brought good news at last. Most of the church had accepted Paul's admonishment, although some holdouts remained. With a grateful heart, but with concern remaining for those continuing to resist, Paul wrote yet another letter to the church, one that was deeply personal, balancing thankfulness to those who had accepted his prior letter with a straightforward defense of his ministry and apostleship to those who continued to rebel. As he wrote, Paul stressed a theme that tied it all together: The church needed to be strong, but not with fortitude the way the world sees it. The strength Paul had in mind would come from the last place one expected to find it.

CHAPTER 1

SALUTATION

From Paul, an apostle of Christ Jesus by the will of God, and Timothy our brother, to the church of God that is in Corinth, with all the saints who are in all Achaia. Grace and peace to you from God our Father and the Lord Jesus Christ!

THANKSGIVING FOR GOD'S COMFORT

Blessed is the God and Father of our Lord Jesus Christ, the Father of mercies and God of all comfort, who comforts us in all our troubles so that we may be able to comfort those experiencing any trouble with the comfort with which we ourselves are comforted by God. For just as the sufferings of Christ overflow toward us, so also our comfort through Christ overflows to you. But if we are afflicted, it is for your comfort and salvation; if we are comforted, it is for your comfort that you experience in your patient endurance of the same sufferings that we also suffer. And our hope for you is steadfast because we know that as you share in our sufferings, so also you will share in our comfort. For we do not want you to be unaware, brothers and sisters, regarding the affliction that happened to us in the province of Asia, that we were burdened excessively, beyond our strength, so that we despaired even of living. Indeed we felt as if the sentence of death had been passed against us, so that we would not trust in ourselves but in God who raises the dead. He delivered us from so great a risk of death, and he will deliver us. We have set our hope on him that he will deliver us yet again, as you also join in helping us by prayer, so that many people may give thanks to God on our behalf for the gracious gift given to us through the help of many.

PAUL DEFENDS HIS CHANGED PLANS

For our reason for confidence is this: The testimony of our conscience, that with pure motives and sincerity which are from God—not by human wisdom but by the grace of God—we conducted ourselves in the world, and all the more toward you. For we do not write you anything other than what you can read and also understand. But I hope that you will understand completely just as also you have partly understood us, that we are your source of pride just as you also are ours in the day of the Lord Jesus. And with this confidence I intended to come to you first so that you would get a second opportunity to see us, and through your help to go on into Macedonia and then from Macedonia to come back to you and be helped on our way into Judea by you. Therefore when I was planning to do this, I did not do so without thinking about what I was doing, did I? Or do I make my plans according to mere human standards so that I would be saying both "Yes, yes" and "No, no" at the same time? But as God is faithful, our message to you is not "Yes" and "No." For the Son of God, Jesus Christ, the one who was proclaimed among you by us—by me and Silvanus and Timothy—was not "Yes" and "No," but it has always been "Yes" in him. For every one of God's promises are "Yes" in him; therefore also through him the "Amen" is spoken, to the glory we give to God. But it is God who establishes us together with you in Christ and who anointed us, who also sealed us and gave us the Spirit in our hearts as a down payment.

WHY PAUL POSTPONED HIS VISIT

Now I appeal to God as my witness, that to spare you I did not come again to Corinth. I do not mean that we rule over your faith, but we are workers with you for your joy, because by faith you stand firm.

CHAPTER 2

So I made up my own mind not to pay you another painful visit. For if I make you sad, who would be left to make me glad but the one I caused to be sad? And I wrote this very thing to you, so that when I came I would not have sadness from those who ought to make me rejoice, since I am confident in you all that my joy would be yours. For out of great distress and anguish of heart I wrote to you with many tears, not to make you sad, but to let you know the love that I have especially for you. But if anyone has caused sadness, he has not saddened me alone, but to some extent (not to exaggerate) he has saddened all of you as well. This punishment on such an individual by the majority is enough for him, so that now instead you should rather forgive and comfort him. This will keep him from being overwhelmed by excessive grief to the point of despair. Therefore I urge you to reaffirm your love for him. For this reason also I wrote you: to test you to see if you are obedient in everything. If you forgive anyone for anything, I also forgive him—for indeed what I have forgiven (if I have forgiven anything) I did so for you in the presence of Christ, so that we may not be exploited by Satan (for we are not ignorant of his schemes). Now when I arrived in Troas to proclaim the gospel of Christ, even though the Lord had opened a door of opportunity for me, I had no relief in my spirit, because I did not find my brother Titus there. So I said goodbye to them and set out for Macedonia.

APOSTOLIC MINISTRY

But thanks be to God who always leads us in triumphal procession in Christ and who makes known through us the fragrance that consists of the knowledge of him in every place. For we are a sweet aroma of Christ to God among those who are being saved and among those who are perishing—to the latter an odor from death to death, but to the former a fragrance from life to life. And who is adequate for these things? For we are not like so many others, hucksters who peddle the word of God for profit, but we are speaking in Christ before God as persons of sincerity, as persons sent from God.

CHAPTER 3

A LIVING LETTER

Are we beginning to commend ourselves again? We don't need letters of recommendation to you or from you as some other people do, do we? You yourselves are our letter, written on our hearts, known and read by everyone, revealing that you are a letter of Christ, delivered by us, written not with ink but by the Spirit of the living God, not *on stone tablets* but on tablets of human hearts.

Now we have such confidence in God through Christ. Not that we are adequate in ourselves to consider anything as if it were coming from ourselves, but our adequacy is from God, who made us adequate to be servants of a new covenant not based on the letter but on the Spirit, for the letter kills, but the Spirit gives life.

THE GREATER GLORY OF THE SPIRIT'S MINISTRY

But if the ministry that produced death—carved in letters *on stone tablets*—came with glory, so that the Israelites could not keep their eyes fixed on the face of Moses because of the glory of his face (a glory which was made ineffective), how much more glorious will the ministry of the Spirit be? For if there was glory in the ministry that produced condemnation, how much more does the ministry that produces righteousness excel in glory! For indeed, what had been glorious now has no glory because of the tremendously greater glory of what replaced it. For if what was made ineffective came with glory, how much more has what remains come in glory! Therefore, since we have such a hope, we behave with great boldness, and not like Moses who used to put a veil over his face to keep the Israelites from staring at the result of the glory that was made ineffective. But their minds were closed. For to this very day, the same veil remains when they hear the old covenant read. It has not been removed because only in Christ is it taken away. But until this very day whenever Moses is read, a veil lies over their minds, but when one turns to the Lord, *the veil is removed.* Now the Lord is the Spirit, and where the Spirit of the Lord is present, there is freedom. And we all, with unveiled faces reflecting the glory of the Lord, are being transformed into the same image from one degree of glory to another, which is from the Lord, who is the Spirit.

CHAPTER 4

PAUL'S PERSEVERANCE IN MINISTRY

Therefore, since we have this ministry, just as God has shown us mercy, we do not become discouraged. But we have rejected shameful hidden deeds, not behaving with deceptiveness or distorting the word of God, but by open proclamation of the truth we commend ourselves to everyone's conscience before God. But even if our gospel is veiled, it is veiled only to those who are perishing, among whom the god of this age has blinded the minds of those who do not believe so they would not see the light of the glorious gospel of Christ, who is the image of God. For we do not proclaim ourselves, but Jesus Christ as Lord, and ourselves as your slaves for Jesus' sake. For God, who said *"Let light shine out of darkness,"* is the one who shined in our hearts to give us the light of the glorious knowledge of God in the face of Christ.

AN ETERNAL WEIGHT OF GLORY

But we have this treasure in clay jars, so that the extraordinary power belongs to God and does not come from us. We are experiencing trouble on every side, but are not crushed; we are perplexed, but not driven to despair; we are persecuted, but not abandoned; we are knocked down, but not destroyed, always carrying around in our body the death of Jesus, so that the life of Jesus may also be made visible in our body. For we who are alive are constantly being handed over to death for Jesus' sake, so that the life of Jesus may also be made visible in our mortal body. As a result, death is at work in us, but life is at work in you. But since we have the same spirit of faith as that shown in what has been written, *"I believed; therefore I spoke,"* we also believe, therefore we also speak. We do so because we know that the one who raised up Jesus will also raise us up with Jesus and will bring us with you into his presence. For all these things are for your sake, so that the grace that is including more and more people may cause thanksgiving to increase to the glory of God. Therefore we do not despair, but even if our physical body is wearing away, our inner person is being renewed day by day. For our momentary, light suffering is producing for us an eternal weight of glory far beyond all comparison because we are not looking at what can be seen but at what cannot be seen. For what can be seen is temporary, but what cannot be seen is eternal.

CHAPTER 5

LIVING BY FAITH, NOT BY SIGHT

For we know that if our earthly house, the tent we live in, is dismantled, we have a building from God, a house not built by human hands, that is eternal in the heavens. For in this earthly house we groan, because we desire to put on our heavenly dwelling, if indeed, after we have put on our heavenly house, we will not be found naked. For we groan while we are in this tent, since we are weighed down, because we do not want to be unclothed, but clothed, so that what is mortal may be swallowed up by life. Now the one who prepared us for this very purpose is God, who gave us the Spirit as a down payment. Therefore we are always full of courage, and we know that as long as we are alive here on earth we are absent from the Lord—for we live by faith, not by sight. Thus we are full of courage and would prefer to be away from the body and at home with the Lord. So then whether we are alive or away, we make it our ambition to please him. For we must all appear before the judgment seat of Christ, so that each one may be paid back according to what he has done while in the body, whether good or evil.

THE MESSAGE OF RECONCILIATION

Therefore, because we know the fear of the Lord, we try to persuade people, but we are well known to God, and I hope we are well known to your consciences too. We are not trying to commend ourselves to you again, but are giving you an opportunity to be proud of us, so that you may be able to answer those who take pride in outward appearance and not in what is in the heart. For if we are out of our minds, it is for God; if we are of sound mind, it is for you. For the love of Christ controls us, since we have concluded this, that Christ died for all; therefore all have died. And he died for all so that those who live should no longer live for themselves but for him who died for them and was raised. So then from now on we acknowledge no one from an outward human point of view. Even though we have known Christ from such a human point of view, now we do not know him in that way any longer. So then, if anyone is in Christ, he is a new creation; what is old has passed away—look, what is new has come! And all these things are from God who reconciled us to himself through Christ and who has given us the ministry of reconciliation. In other words, in Christ God was reconciling the world to himself, not counting people's trespasses against them, and he has given us the message of reconciliation. Therefore we are ambassadors for Christ, as though God were making his plea through us. We plead with you on Christ's behalf, "Be reconciled to God!" God made the one who did not know sin to be sin for us, so that in him we would become the righteousness of God.

CHAPTER 6

GOD'S SUFFERING SERVANTS

Now because we are fellow workers, we also urge you not to receive the grace of God in vain. For he says, *"I heard you at the acceptable time, and in the day of salvation I helped you."* Look, now is *the acceptable time;* look, now is *the day of salvation!* We do not give anyone an occasion for taking an offense in anything, so that no fault may be found with our ministry. But as God's servants, we have commended ourselves in every way, with great endurance, in persecutions, in difficulties, in distresses, in beatings, in imprisonments, in riots, in troubles, in sleepless nights, in hunger, by purity, by knowledge, by patience, by benevolence, by the Holy Spirit, by genuine love, by truthful teaching, by the power of God, with weapons of righteousness both for the right hand and for the left, through glory and dishonor, through slander and praise; regarded as impostors, and yet true; as unknown, and yet well-known; as dying and yet—see!—we continue to live; as those who are scourged and yet not executed; as sorrowful, but always rejoicing; as poor, but making many rich; as having nothing, and yet possessing everything.

We have spoken freely to you, Corinthians; our heart has been opened wide to you. Our affection for you is not restricted, but you are restricted in your affections for us. Now as a fair exchange—I speak as to my children—open wide your hearts to us also.

UNEQUAL PARTNERS

Do not become partners with those who do not believe, for what partnership is there between righteousness and lawlessness, or what fellowship does light have with darkness? And what agreement does Christ have with Beliar? Or what does a believer share in common with an unbeliever? And what mutual agreement does the temple of God have with idols? For we are the temple of the living God, just as God said, *"I will live in them and will walk among them, and I will be their God, and they will be my people."* Therefore *"come out from their midst, and be separate,"* says the Lord, *"and touch no unclean thing, and I will welcome you, and I will be a father to you, and you will be my sons and daughters,"* says the All-Powerful Lord.

CHAPTER 7

SELF-PURIFICATION

Therefore, since we have these promises, dear friends, let us cleanse ourselves from everything that could defile the body and the spirit, and thus accomplish holiness out of reverence for God. Make room for us in your hearts; we have wronged no one; we have ruined no one; we have exploited no one. I do not say this to condemn you, for I told you before that you are in our hearts so that we die together and live together with you.

A LETTER THAT CAUSED SADNESS

I have great confidence in you; I take great pride on your behalf. I am filled with encouragement; I am overflowing with joy in the midst of all our suffering. For even when we came into Macedonia, our body had no rest at all, but we were troubled in every way—struggles from the outside, fears from within. But God, who encourages the downhearted, encouraged us by the arrival of Titus. We were encouraged not only by his arrival, but also by the encouragement you gave him, as he reported to us your longing, your mourning, your deep concern for me, so that I rejoiced more than ever. For even if I made you sad by my letter, I do not regret having written it (even though I did regret it, for I see that my letter made you sad, though only for a short time). Now I rejoice, not because you were made sad, but because you were made sad to the point of repentance. For you were made sad as God intended, so that you were not harmed in any way by us. For sadness as intended by God produces a repentance that leads to salvation, leaving no regret, but worldly sadness brings about death. For see what this very thing, this sadness as God intended, has produced in you: what eagerness, what defense of yourselves, what indignation, what alarm, what longing, what deep concern, what punishment! In everything you have proved yourselves to be innocent in this matter. So then, even though I wrote to you, it was not on account of the one who did wrong or on account of the one who was wronged, but to reveal to you your eagerness on our behalf before God. Therefore we have been encouraged. And in addition to our own encouragement, we rejoiced even more at the joy of Titus because all of you have refreshed his spirit. For if I have boasted to him about anything concerning you, I have not been embarrassed by you, but just as everything we said to you was true, so our boasting to Titus about you has proved true as well. And his affection for you is much greater when he remembers the obedience of you all, how you welcomed him with fear and trembling. I rejoice because in everything I am fully confident in you.

CHAPTER 8

COMPLETING THE COLLECTION FOR THE SAINTS

Now we make known to you, brothers and sisters, the grace of God given to the churches of Macedonia, that during a severe ordeal of suffering, their abundant joy and their extreme poverty have overflowed in the wealth of their generosity. For I testify, they gave according to their means and beyond their means. They did so voluntarily, begging us with great earnestness for the blessing and fellowship of helping the saints. And they did this not just as we had hoped, but they gave themselves first to the Lord and to us by the will of God. Thus we urged Titus that, just as he had previously begun this work, so also he should complete this act of kindness for you. But as you excel in everything—in faith, in speech, in knowledge, and in all eagerness and in the love from us that is in you—make sure that you excel in this act of kindness too. I am not saying this as a command, but I am testing the genuineness of your love by comparison with the eagerness of others. For you know the grace of our Lord Jesus Christ, that although he was rich, he became poor for your sakes, so that you by his poverty could become rich. So here is my opinion on this matter: It is to your advantage, since you made a good start last year both in your giving and your desire to give, to finish what you started, so that just as you wanted to do it eagerly, you can also complete it according to your means. For if the eagerness is present, the gift itself is acceptable according to whatever one has, not according to what he does not have. For I do not say this so there would be relief for others and suffering for you, but as a matter of equality. At the present time, your abundance will meet their need, so that one day their abundance may also meet your need, and thus there may be equality, as it is written: *"The one who gathered much did not have too much, and the one who gathered little did not have too little."*

THE MISSION OF TITUS

But thanks be to God who put in the heart of Titus the same devotion I have for you, because he not only accepted our request, but since he was very eager, he is coming to you of his own accord. And we are sending along with him the brother who is praised by all the churches for his work in spreading the gospel. In addition, this brother has also been chosen by the churches as our traveling companion as we administer this generous gift to the glory of the Lord himself and to show our readiness to help. We did this as a precaution so that no one should blame us in regard to this generous gift we are administering. For we are *concerned about what is right not only before the Lord but also before men.* And we are sending with them our brother whom we have tested many times and found eager in many matters, but who now is much more eager than ever because of the great confidence he has in you. If there is any question about Titus, he is my partner and fellow worker among you; if there is any question about our brothers, they are messengers of the churches, a glory to Christ. Therefore show them openly before the churches the proof of your love and of our pride in you.

CHAPTER 9

PREPARING THE GIFT

For it is not necessary for me to write you about this service to the saints because I know your eagerness to help. I keep boasting to the Macedonians about this eagerness of yours, that Achaia has been ready to give since last year, and your zeal to participate has stirred up most of them. But I am sending these brothers so that our boasting about you may not be empty in this case, so that you may be ready just as I kept telling them. For if any of the Macedonians should come with me and find that you are not ready to give, we would be humiliated (not to mention you) by this confidence we had in you. Therefore I thought it necessary to urge these brothers to go to you in advance and to arrange ahead of time the generous contribution you had promised, so this may be ready as a generous gift and not as something you feel forced to do. My point is this: The person who sows sparingly will also reap sparingly, and the person who sows generously will also reap generously. Each one of you should give just as he has decided in his heart, not reluctantly or under compulsion, because God loves a cheerful giver. And God is able to make all grace overflow to you so that because you have enough of everything in every way at all times, you will overflow in every good work. Just as it is written, *"He has scattered widely, he has given to the poor; his righteousness remains forever."* Now God who provides seed for the sower and bread for food will provide and multiply your supply of seed and will cause the harvest of your righteousness to grow. You will be enriched in every way so that you may be generous on every occasion, which is producing through us thanksgiving to God, because the service of this ministry is not only providing for the needs of the saints but is also overflowing with many thanks to God. Through the evidence of this service they will glorify God because of your obedience to your confession in the gospel of Christ and the generosity of your sharing with them and with everyone. And in their prayers on your behalf, they long for you because of the extraordinary grace God has shown to you. Thanks be to God for his indescribable gift!

CHAPTER 10

PAUL'S AUTHORITY FROM THE LORD

Now I, Paul, appeal to you personally by the meekness and gentleness of Christ (I who am meek when present among you, but am full of courage toward you when away!)—now I ask that when I am present I may not have to be bold with the confidence that (I expect) I will dare to use against some who consider us to be behaving according to human standards. For though we live as human beings, we do not wage war according to human standards, for the weapons of our warfare are not human weapons, but are made powerful by God for tearing down strongholds. We tear down arguments and every arrogant obstacle that is raised up against the knowledge of God, and we take every thought captive to make it obey Christ. We are also ready to punish every act of disobedience, whenever your obedience is complete. You are looking at outward appearances. If anyone is confident that he belongs to Christ, he should reflect on this again: Just as he himself belongs to Christ, so too do we. For if I boast somewhat more about our authority that the Lord gave us for building you up and not for tearing you down, I will not be ashamed of doing so. I do not want to seem as though I am trying to terrify you with my letters, because some say, "His letters are weighty and forceful, but his physical presence is weak and his speech is of no account." Let such a person consider this: What we say by letters when we are absent, we also are in actions when we are present.

PAUL'S MISSION

For we would not dare to classify or compare ourselves with some of those who recommend themselves. But when they measure themselves by themselves and compare themselves with themselves, they are without understanding. But we will not boast beyond certain limits, but will confine our boasting according to the limits of the work to which God has appointed us, that reaches even as far as you. For we were not over-extending ourselves, as though we did not reach as far as you, because we were the first to reach as far as you with the gospel about Christ. Nor do we boast beyond certain limits in the work done by others, but we hope that as your faith continues to grow, our work may be greatly expanded among you according to our limits, so that we may preach the gospel in the regions that lie beyond you, and not boast of work already done in another person's area. But *the one who boasts must boast in the Lord.* For it is not the person who commends himself who is approved, but the person the Lord commends.

CHAPTER 11

PAUL AND HIS OPPONENTS

I wish that you would be patient with me in a little foolishness, but indeed you are being patient with me! For I am jealous for you with godly jealousy, because I promised you in marriage to one husband, to present you as a pure virgin to Christ. But I am afraid that just as the serpent deceived Eve by his treachery, your minds may be led astray from a sincere and pure devotion to Christ. For if someone comes and proclaims another Jesus different from the one we proclaimed, or if you receive a different spirit than the one you received, or a different gospel than the one you accepted, you put up with it well enough! For I consider myself not at all inferior to those "super-apostles." And even if I am unskilled in speaking, yet I am certainly not so in knowledge. Indeed, we have made this plain to you in everything in every way. Or did I commit a sin by humbling myself so that you could be exalted, because I proclaimed the gospel of God to you free of charge? I robbed other churches by receiving support from them so that I could serve you! When I was with you and was in need, I was not a burden to anyone, for the brothers who came from Macedonia fully supplied my needs. I kept myself from being a burden to you in any way, and will continue to do so. As the truth of Christ is in me, this boasting of mine will not be stopped in the regions of Achaia. Why? Because I do not love you? God knows I do! And what I am doing I will continue to do, so that I may eliminate any opportunity for those who want a chance to be regarded as our equals in the things they boast about. For such people are false apostles, deceitful workers, disguising themselves as apostles of Christ. And no wonder, for even Satan disguises himself as an angel of light. Therefore it is not surprising his servants also disguise themselves as servants of righteousness, whose end will correspond to their actions.

PAUL'S SUFFERINGS FOR CHRIST

I say again, let no one think that I am a fool. But if you do, then at least accept me as a fool, so that I too may boast a little. What I am saying with this boastful confidence I do not say the way the Lord would. Instead it is, as it were, foolishness. Since many are boasting according to human standards, I too will boast. For since you are so wise, you put up with fools gladly. For you put up with it if someone makes slaves of you, if someone exploits you, if someone takes advantage of you, if someone behaves arrogantly toward you, if someone strikes you in the face. (To my disgrace I must say that we were too weak for that!) But whatever anyone else dares to boast about (I am speaking foolishly), I also dare to boast about the same thing. Are they Hebrews? So am I. Are they Israelites? So am I. Are they descendants of Abraham? So am I. Are they servants of Christ? (I am talking like I am out of my mind!) I am even more so: with much greater labors, with far more imprisonments, with more severe beatings, facing death many times. Five times I received from the Jews forty lashes less one. Three times I was beaten with a rod. Once I received a stoning. Three times I suffered shipwreck. A night and a day I spent adrift in the open sea. I have been on journeys many times, in dangers from rivers, in dangers from robbers, in dangers from my own countrymen, in dangers from Gentiles, in dangers in the city, in dangers in the wilderness, in dangers at sea, in dangers from false brothers, in hard work and toil, through many sleepless nights, in hunger and thirst, many times without food, in cold and without enough clothing. Apart from other things, there is the daily pressure on me of my anxious concern for all the churches. Who is weak, and I am not weak? Who is led into sin, and I do not burn with indignation? If I must boast, I will boast about the things that show my weakness. The God and Father of the Lord Jesus, who is blessed forever, knows I am not lying. In Damascus, the governor under King Aretas was guarding the city of Damascus in order to arrest me, but I was let down in a rope-basket through a window in the city wall, and escaped his hands.

CHAPTER 12

PAUL'S THORN IN THE FLESH

It is necessary to go on boasting. Though it is not profitable, I will go on to visions and revelations from the Lord. I know a man in Christ who fourteen years ago (whether in the body or out of the body I do not know, God knows) was caught up to the third heaven. And I know that this man (whether in the body or apart from the body I do not know, God knows) was caught up into paradise and heard things too sacred to be put into words, things that a person is not permitted to speak. On behalf of such an individual I will boast, but on my own behalf I will not boast, except about my weaknesses. For even if I wish to boast, I will not be a fool, for I would be telling the truth, but I refrain from this so that no one may regard me beyond what he sees in me or what he hears from me, even because of the extraordinary character of the revelations. Therefore, so that I would not become arrogant, a thorn in the flesh was given to me, a messenger of Satan to trouble me—so that I would not become arrogant. I asked the Lord three times about this, that it would depart from me. But he said to me, "My grace is enough for you, for my power is made perfect in weakness." So then, I will boast most gladly about my weaknesses, so that the power of Christ may reside in me. Therefore I am content with weaknesses, with insults, with troubles, with persecutions and difficulties for the sake of Christ, for whenever I am weak, then I am strong.

THE SIGNS OF AN APOSTLE

I have become a fool. You yourselves forced me to do it, for I should have been commended by you. For I lack nothing in comparison to those "super-apostles," even though I am nothing. Indeed, the signs of an apostle were performed among you with great perseverance by signs and wonders and powerful deeds. For how were you treated worse than the other churches, except that I myself was not a burden to you? Forgive me this injustice! Look, for the third time I am ready to come to you, and I will not be a burden to you, because I do not want your possessions, but you. For children should not have to save up for their parents, but parents for their children. Now I will most gladly spend and be spent for your lives! If I love you more, am I to be loved less? But be that as it may, I have not burdened you. Yet because I was a crafty person, I took you in by deceit! I have not taken advantage of you through anyone I have sent to you, have I? I urged Titus to visit you, and I sent our brother along with him. Titus did not take advantage of you, did he? Did we not conduct ourselves in the same spirit? Did we not behave in the same way? Have you been thinking all this time that we have been defending ourselves to you? We are speaking in Christ before God, and everything we do, dear friends, is to build you up. For I am afraid that somehow when I come I will not find you what I wish, and you will find me not what you wish. I am afraid that somehow there may be quarreling, jealousy, intense anger, selfish ambition, slander, gossip, arrogance, and disorder. I am afraid that when I come again, my God may humiliate me before you, and I will grieve for many of those who previously sinned and have not repented of the impurity, sexual immorality, and licentiousness that they have practiced.

CHAPTER 13

PAUL'S THIRD VISIT TO CORINTH

This is the third time I am coming to visit you. *By the testimony of two or three witnesses every matter will be established.* I said before when I was present the second time and now, though absent, I say again to those who sinned previously and to all the rest, that if I come again, I will not spare anyone, since you are demanding proof that Christ is speaking through me. He is not weak toward you but is powerful among you. For indeed he was crucified by reason of weakness, but he lives because of God's power. For we also are weak in him, but we will live together with him, because of God's power toward you. Put yourselves to the test to see if you are in the faith; examine yourselves! Or do you not recognize regarding yourselves that Jesus Christ is in you—unless, indeed, you fail the test! And I hope that you will realize that we have not failed the test! Now we pray to God that you may not do anything wrong, not so that we may appear to have passed the test, but so that you may do what is right even if we may appear to have failed the test. For we cannot do anything against the truth, but only for the sake of the truth. For we rejoice whenever we are weak, but you are strong. And we pray for this: that you may become fully qualified. Because of this I am writing these things while absent, so that when I arrive I may not have to deal harshly with you by using my authority—the Lord gave it to me for building up, not for tearing down!

FINAL EXHORTATIONS AND GREETINGS

Finally, brothers and sisters, rejoice, set things right, be encouraged, agree with one another, live in peace, and the God of love and peace will be with you. Greet one another with a holy kiss. All the saints greet you. The grace of the Lord Jesus Christ and the love of God and the fellowship of the Holy Spirit be with you all.

GALATIANS

PROLOGUE

During their first missionary journey, Paul and Barnabas had planted several churches in Galatia, a region of Asia Minor or modern Turkey. Now Paul heard that these churches were struggling. False teachers claimed that following Jesus was not enough. They declared that believers had to follow Old Testament law as well.

In response Paul wrote one of his first letters. His message was clear and emphatic: The gospel is a message of grace. It is a message of Christ and what *he* has done. Jesus plus anything does not equal the gospel—and that includes the law. God had given the law for a purpose, but that was fulfilled in Jesus.

What concerned Paul most was how easily the Galatian believers had been confused. Paul knew that the church had been established on the gospel. How could it depart so soon from the solid foundation he had helped lay? He needed to remind the Galatians that following Christ meant freedom. But he also had to ensure that they rightly understood what this freedom meant. Yes, it meant freedom from the law, but Jesus provided an even greater freedom than that.

CHAPTER 1

SALUTATION

From Paul, an apostle (not from men, nor by human agency, but by Jesus Christ and God the Father who raised him from the dead) and all the brothers with me, to the churches of Galatia. Grace and peace to you from God the Father and our Lord Jesus Christ, who gave himself for our sins to rescue us from this present evil age according to the will of our God and Father, to whom be glory forever and ever! Amen.

OCCASION OF THE LETTER

I am astonished that you are so quickly deserting the one who called you by the grace of Christ and are following a different gospel—not that there really is another gospel, but there are some who are disturbing you and wanting to distort the gospel of Christ. But even if we (or an angel from heaven) should preach a gospel contrary to the one we preached to you, let him be condemned to hell! As we have said before, and now I say again, if any one is preaching to you a gospel contrary to what you received, let him be condemned to hell! Am I now trying to gain the approval of people, or of God? Or am I trying to please people? If I were still trying to please people, I would not be a slave of Christ!

PAUL'S VINDICATION OF HIS APOSTLESHIP

Now I want you to know, brothers and sisters, that the gospel I preached is not of human origin. For I did not receive it or learn it from any human source; instead I received it by a revelation of Jesus Christ.

For you have heard of my former way of life in Judaism, how I was savagely persecuting the church of God and trying to destroy it. I was advancing in Judaism beyond many of my contemporaries in my nation, and was extremely zealous for the traditions of my ancestors. But when the one who set me apart from birth and called me by his grace was pleased to reveal his Son in me so that I could preach him among the Gentiles, I did not go to ask advice from any human being, nor did I go up to Jerusalem to see those who were apostles before me, but right away I departed to Arabia, and then returned to Damascus.

Then after three years I went up to Jerusalem to visit Cephas and get information from him, and I stayed with him fifteen days. But I saw none of the other apostles except James the Lord's brother. I assure you that, before God, I am not lying about what I am writing to you! Afterward I went to the regions of Syria and Cilicia. But I was personally unknown to the churches of Judea that are in Christ. They were only hearing, "The one who once persecuted us is now proclaiming the good news of the faith he once tried to destroy." So they glorified God because of me.

CHAPTER 2

CONFIRMATION FROM THE JERUSALEM APOSTLES

Then after fourteen years I went up to Jerusalem again with Barnabas, taking Titus along too. I went there because of a revelation and presented to them the gospel that I preach among the Gentiles. But I did so only in a private meeting with the influential people, to make sure that I was not running—or had not run—in vain. Yet not even Titus, who was with me, was compelled to be circumcised, although he was a Greek. Now this matter arose because of the false brothers with false pretenses who slipped in unnoticed to spy on our freedom that we have in Christ Jesus, to make us slaves. But we did not surrender to them even for a moment, in order that the truth of the gospel would remain with you.

But from those who were influential (whatever they were makes no difference to me; God shows no favoritism between people)— those influential leaders added nothing to my message. On the contrary, when they saw that I was entrusted with the gospel to the uncircumcised just as Peter was entrusted with the gospel to the circumcised (for he who empowered Peter for his apostleship to the circumcised also empowered me for my apostleship to the Gentiles) and when James, Cephas, and John, who had a reputation as pillars, recognized the grace that had been given to me, they gave to Barnabas and me the right hand of fellowship, agreeing that we would go to the Gentiles and they to the circumcised. They requested only that we remember the poor, the very thing I also was eager to do.

PAUL REBUKES PETER

But when Cephas came to Antioch, I opposed him to his face, because he had clearly done wrong. Until certain people came from James, he had been eating with the Gentiles. But when they arrived, he stopped doing this and separated himself because he was afraid of those who were pro-circumcision. And the rest of the Jews also joined with him in this hypocrisy, so that even Barnabas was led astray with them by their hypocrisy. But when I saw that they were not behaving consistently with the truth of the gospel, I said to Cephas in front of them all, "If you, although you are a Jew, live like a Gentile and not like a Jew, how can you try to force the Gentiles to live like Jews?"

THE JUSTIFICATION OF JEWS AND GENTILES

We are Jews by birth and not Gentile sinners, yet we know that no one is justified by the works of the law but by the faithfulness of Jesus Christ. And we have come to believe in Christ Jesus, so that we may be justified by the faithfulness of Christ and not by the works of the law, because by the works of the law no one will be justified. But if while seeking to be justified in Christ we ourselves have also been found to be sinners, is Christ then one who encourages sin? Absolutely not! But if I build up again those things I once destroyed, I demonstrate that I am one who breaks God's law. For through the law I died to the law so that I may live to God. I have been crucified with Christ, and it is no longer I who live, but Christ lives in me. So the life I now live in the body, I live because of the faithfulness of the Son of God, who loved me and gave himself for me. I do not set aside God's grace, because if righteousness could come through the law, then Christ died for nothing!

CHAPTER 3

JUSTIFICATION BY LAW OR BY FAITH?

You foolish Galatians! Who has cast a spell on you? Before your eyes Jesus Christ was vividly portrayed as crucified! The only thing I want to learn from you is this: Did you receive the Spirit by doing the works of the law or by believing what you heard? Are you so foolish?

Although you began with the Spirit, are you now trying to finish by human effort? Have you suffered so many things for nothing?—if indeed it was for nothing. Does God then give you the Spirit and work miracles among you by your doing the works of the law or by your believing what you heard?

Just as Abraham *believed God, and it was credited to him as righteousness,* so then, understand that those who believe are the sons of Abraham. And the scripture, foreseeing that God would justify the Gentiles by faith, proclaimed the gospel to Abraham ahead of time, saying, "*All the nations will be blessed in you.*" So then those who believe are blessed along with Abraham the believer. For all who rely on doing the works of the law are under a curse because it is written, "*Cursed is everyone who does not keep on doing everything written in the book of the law.*" Now it is clear no one is justified before God by the law because *the righteous one will live by faith.* But the law is not based on faith, but *the one who does* the works of the law *will live by them.* Christ redeemed us from the curse of the law by becoming a curse for us (because it is written, "*Cursed is everyone who hangs on a tree*") in order that in Christ Jesus the blessing of Abraham would come to the Gentiles, so that we could receive the promise of the Spirit by faith.

INHERITANCE COMES FROM PROMISES AND NOT LAW

Brothers and sisters, I offer an example from everyday life: When a covenant has been ratified, even though it is only a human contract, no one can set it aside or add anything to it. Now the promises were spoken to Abraham and to his descendant. Scripture does not say, "and to the descendants," referring to many, but *"and to your descendant,"* referring to one, who is Christ. What I am saying is this: The law that came 430 years later does not cancel a covenant previously ratified by God, so as to invalidate the promise. For if the inheritance is based on the law, it is no longer based on the promise, but God graciously gave it to Abraham through the promise.

Why then was the law given? It was added because of transgressions, until the arrival of the descendant to whom the promise had been made. It was administered through angels by an intermediary. Now an intermediary is not for one party alone, but God is one. Is the law therefore opposed to the promises of God? Absolutely not! For if a law had been given that was able to give life, then righteousness would certainly have come by the law. But the scripture imprisoned everything under sin so that the promise could be given—because of the faithfulness of Jesus Christ—to those who believe.

SONS OF GOD ARE HEIRS OF PROMISE

Now before faith came we were held in custody under the law, being kept as prisoners until the coming faith would be revealed. Thus the law had become our guardian until Christ, so that we could be declared righteous by faith. But now that faith has come, we are no longer under a guardian. For in Christ Jesus you are all sons of God through faith. For all of you who were baptized into Christ have clothed yourselves with Christ. There is neither Jew nor Greek, there is neither slave nor free, there is neither male nor female—for all of you are one in Christ Jesus. And if you belong to Christ, then you are Abraham's descendants, heirs according to the promise.

CHAPTER 4

Now I mean that the heir, as long as he is a minor, is no different from a slave, though he is the owner of everything. But he is under guardians and managers until the date set by his father. So also we, when we were minors, were enslaved under the basic forces of the world. But when the appropriate time had come, God sent out his Son, born of a woman, born under the law, to redeem those who were under the law, so that we may be adopted as sons with full rights. And because you are sons, God sent the Spirit of his Son into our hearts, who calls "*Abba!* Father!" So you are no longer a slave but a son, and if you are a son, then you are also an heir through God.

HEIRS OF PROMISE ARE NOT
TO RETURN TO LAW

Formerly when you did not know God, you were enslaved to beings that by nature are not gods at all. But now that you have come to know God (or rather to be known by God), how can you turn back again to the weak and worthless basic forces? Do you want to be enslaved to them all over again? You are observing religious days and months and seasons and years. I fear for you that my work for you may have been in vain. I beg you, brothers and sisters, become like me, because I have become like you. You have done me no wrong!

PERSONAL APPEAL OF PAUL

But you know it was because of a physical illness that I first proclaimed the gospel to you, and though my physical condition put you to the test, you did not despise or reject me. Instead, you welcomed me as though I were an angel of God, as though I were Christ Jesus himself! Where then is your sense of happiness now? For I testify about you that if it were possible, you would have pulled out your eyes and given them to me! So then, have I become your enemy by telling you the truth?

They court you eagerly, but for no good purpose; they want to exclude you, so that you would seek them eagerly. However, it is good to be sought eagerly for a good purpose at all times, and not only when I am present with you. My children—I am again undergoing birth pains until Christ is formed in you! I wish I could be with you now and change my tone of voice, because I am perplexed about you.

AN APPEAL FROM ALLEGORY

Tell me, you who want to be under the law, do you not understand the law? For it is written that Abraham had two sons, one by the slave woman and the other by the free woman. But one, the son by the slave woman, was born by natural descent, while the other, the son by the free woman, was born through the promise. These things may be treated as an allegory, for these women represent two covenants. One is from Mount Sinai bearing children for slavery; this is Hagar. Now Hagar represents Mount Sinai in Arabia and corresponds to the present Jerusalem, for she is in slavery with her children. But the Jerusalem above is free, and she is our mother. For it is written:

> *"Rejoice, O barren woman who does not bear children;*
> *break forth and shout, you who have no birth pains,*
> *because the children of the desolate woman are more numerous*
> *than those of the woman who has a husband."*

But you, brothers and sisters, are children of the promise like Isaac. But just as at that time the one born by natural descent persecuted the one born according to the Spirit, so it is now. But what does the scripture say? *"Throw out the slave woman and her son, for the son of the slave woman will not share the inheritance with the son"* of the free woman. Therefore, brothers and sisters, we are not children of the slave woman but of the free woman.

CHAPTER 5

FREEDOM OF THE BELIEVER

For freedom Christ has set us free. Stand firm, then, and do not be subject again to the yoke of slavery. Listen! I, Paul, tell you that if you let yourselves be circumcised, Christ will be of no benefit to you at all! And I testify again to every man who lets himself be circumcised that he is obligated to obey the whole law. You who are trying to be declared righteous by the law have been alienated from Christ; you have fallen away from grace! For through the Spirit, by faith, we wait expectantly for the hope of righteousness. For in Christ Jesus neither circumcision nor uncircumcision carries any weight—the only thing that matters is faith working through love.

You were running well; who prevented you from obeying the truth? This persuasion does not come from the one who calls you! A little yeast makes the whole batch of dough rise! I am confident in the Lord that you will accept no other view. But the one who is confusing you will pay the penalty, whoever he may be. Now, brothers and sisters, if I am still preaching circumcision, why am I still being persecuted? In that case the offense of the cross has been removed. I wish those agitators would go so far as to castrate themselves!

PRACTICE LOVE

For you were called to freedom, brothers and sisters; only do not use your freedom as an opportunity to indulge your flesh, but through love serve one another. For the whole law can be summed up in a single commandment, namely, *"You must love your neighbor as yourself."* However, if you continually bite and devour one another, beware that you are not consumed by one another. But I say, live by the Spirit and you will not carry out the desires of the flesh. For the flesh has desires that are opposed to the Spirit, and the Spirit has desires that are opposed to the flesh, for these are in opposition to each other, so that you cannot do what you want. But if you are led by the Spirit, you are not under the law. Now the works of the flesh are obvious: sexual immorality, impurity, depravity, idolatry, sorcery, hostilities, strife, jealousy, outbursts of anger, selfish rivalries, dissensions, factions, envying, murder, drunkenness, carousing, and similar things. I am warning you, as I had warned you before: Those who practice such things will not inherit the kingdom of God!

But the fruit of the Spirit is love, joy, peace, patience, kindness, goodness, faithfulness, gentleness, and self-control. Against such things there is no law. Now those who belong to Christ have crucified the flesh with its passions and desires. If we live by the Spirit, let us also behave in accordance with the Spirit. Let us not become conceited, provoking one another, being jealous of one another.

CHAPTER 6

SUPPORT ONE ANOTHER

Brothers and sisters, if a person is discovered in some sin, you who are spiritual restore such a person in a spirit of gentleness. Pay close attention to yourselves, so that you are not tempted too. Carry one another's burdens, and in this way you will fulfill the law of Christ. For if anyone thinks he is something when he is nothing, he deceives himself. Let each one examine his own work. Then he can take pride in himself and not compare himself with someone else. For each one will carry his own load.

Now the one who receives instruction in the word must share all good things with the one who teaches it. Do not be deceived. God will not be made a fool. For a person will reap what he sows, because the person who sows to his own flesh will reap corruption from the flesh, but the one who sows to the Spirit will reap eternal life from the Spirit. So we must not grow weary in doing good, for in due time we will reap, if we do not give up. So then, whenever we have an opportunity, let us do good to all people, and especially to those who belong to the family of faith.

FINAL INSTRUCTIONS AND BENEDICTION

See what big letters I make as I write to you with my own hand!

Those who want to make a good showing in external matters are trying to force you to be circumcised. They do so only to avoid being persecuted for the cross of Christ. For those who are circumcised do not obey the law themselves, but they want you to be circumcised so that they can boast about your flesh. But may I never boast except in the cross of our Lord Jesus Christ, through which the world has been crucified to me, and I to the world. For neither circumcision nor uncircumcision counts for anything; the only thing that matters is a new creation! And all who will behave in accordance with this rule, peace and mercy be on them, and on the Israel of God.

From now on let no one cause me trouble, for I bear the marks of Jesus on my body.

The grace of our Lord Jesus Christ be with your spirit, brothers and sisters. Amen.

EPHESIANS

PROLOGUE

Ephesus was an important city, the third largest in the Roman Empire. The church in this city was quite strategic, much like the one in Rome. A strong Ephesian church could foster a strong church in the region, which eventually could prompt a strong church reaching all the way to the ends of the earth.

But just because a church was located in an influential city did not mean it would automatically be just as significant. Paul knew that the Ephesians, like the Romans, needed to remember the fundamentals of the faith. Without that firm foundation, the church would have nothing to stand on. But that wasn't all.

They also required a reminder to live out what they believed. Faith is most noticeable when it is seen, not just heard. But there was still one final key Paul knew that the Ephesians lacked. What Paul called the church to do could not be accomplished by any single believer alone. Churches are made of many different people for a reason. And Paul was going to be sure that the church understood that reason.

CHAPTER 1

SALUTATION

From Paul, an apostle of Christ Jesus by the will of God, to the saints [in Ephesus], the faithful in Christ Jesus. Grace and peace to you from God our Father and the Lord Jesus Christ!

SPIRITUAL BLESSINGS IN CHRIST

Blessed is the God and Father of our Lord Jesus Christ, who has blessed us with every spiritual blessing in the heavenly realms in Christ. For he chose us in Christ before the foundation of the world that we should be holy and blameless before him in love. He did this by predestining us to adoption as his legal heirs through Jesus Christ, according to the pleasure of his will—to the praise of the glory of his grace that he has freely bestowed on us in his dearly loved Son. In him we have redemption through his blood, the forgiveness of our offenses, according to the riches of his grace that he lavished on us in all wisdom and insight. He did this when he revealed to us the mystery of his will, according to his good pleasure that he set forth in Christ, toward the administration of the fullness of the times, to head up all things in Christ—the things in heaven and the things on earth. In Christ we too have been claimed as God's own possession, since we were predestined according to the purpose of him who accomplishes all things according to the counsel of his will so that we, who were the first to set our hope on Christ, would be to the praise of his glory. And when you heard the word of truth (the gospel of your salvation)—when you believed in Christ—you were marked with the seal of the promised Holy Spirit, who is the down payment of our inheritance, until the redemption of God's own possession, to the praise of his glory.

PRAYER FOR WISDOM AND REVELATION

For this reason, because I have heard of your faith in the Lord Jesus and your love for all the saints, I do not cease to give thanks for you when I remember you in my prayers. I pray that the God of our Lord Jesus Christ, the glorious Father, will give you spiritual wisdom and revelation in your growing knowledge of him, —since the eyes of your heart have been enlightened—so that you can know what is the hope of his calling, what is the wealth of his glorious inheritance in the saints, and what is the incomparable greatness of his power toward us who believe, as displayed in the exercise of his immense strength. This power he exercised in Christ when he raised him from the dead and seated him at his right hand in the heavenly realms far above every rule and authority and power and dominion and every name that is named, not only in this age but also in the one to come. And God *put all things under* Christ's *feet,* and gave him to the church as head over all things. Now the church is his body, the fullness of him who fills all in all.

CHAPTER 2

NEW LIFE INDIVIDUALLY

And although you were dead in your offenses and sins, in which you formerly lived according to this world's present path, according to the ruler of the domain of the air, the ruler of the spirit that is now energizing the sons of disobedience, among whom all of us also formerly lived out our lives in the cravings of our flesh, indulging the desires of the flesh and the mind, and were by nature children of wrath even as the rest...

But God, being rich in mercy because of his great love with which he loved us, even though we were dead in offenses, made us alive together with Christ—by grace you are saved!—and he raised us up together with him and seated us together with him in the heavenly realms in Christ Jesus, to demonstrate in the coming ages the surpassing wealth of his grace in kindness toward us in Christ Jesus. For by grace you are saved through faith, and this is not from yourselves, it is the gift of God; it is not from works, so that no one can boast. For we are his creative work, having been created in Christ Jesus for good works that God prepared beforehand so we can do them.

NEW LIFE CORPORATELY

Therefore remember that formerly you, the Gentiles in the flesh—who are called "uncircumcision" by the so-called "circumcision" that is performed on the body by human hands—that you were at that time without the Messiah, alienated from the citizenship of Israel and strangers to the covenants of promise, having no hope and without God in the world. But now in Christ Jesus you who used to be far away have been brought near by the blood of Christ. For he is our peace, the one who made both groups into one and who destroyed the middle wall of partition, the hostility, when he nullified in his flesh the law of commandments in decrees. He did this to create in himself one new man out of two, thus making peace, and to reconcile them both in one body to God through the cross, by which the hostility has been killed. And he came and preached peace to you who were far off and peace to those who were near, so that through him we both have access in one Spirit to the Father. So then you are no longer foreigners and noncitizens, but you are fellow citizens with the saints and members of God's household, because you have been built on the foundation of the apostles and prophets, with Christ Jesus himself as the cornerstone. In him the whole building, being joined together, grows into a holy temple in the Lord, in whom you also are being built together into a dwelling place of God in the Spirit.

CHAPTER 3

PAUL'S RELATIONSHIP
TO THE DIVINE MYSTERY

For this reason I, Paul, the prisoner of Christ Jesus for the sake of you Gentiles if indeed you have heard of the stewardship of God's grace that was given to me for you, that by revelation the mystery was made known to me, as I wrote before briefly. When reading this, you will be able to understand my insight into the mystery of Christ (which was not disclosed to people in former generations as it has now been revealed to his holy apostles and prophets by the Spirit), namely, that through the gospel the Gentiles are fellow heirs, fellow members of the body, and fellow partakers of the promise in Christ Jesus. I became a servant of this gospel according to the gift of God's grace that was given to me by the exercise of his power. To me—less than the least of all the saints—this grace was given, to proclaim to the Gentiles the unfathomable riches of Christ and to enlighten everyone about God's secret plan—the mystery that has been hidden for ages in God who has created all things. The purpose of this enlightenment is that through the church the multifaceted wisdom of God should now be disclosed to the rulers and the authorities in the heavenly realms. This was according to the eternal purpose that he accomplished in Christ Jesus our Lord, in whom we have boldness and confident access to God by way of Christ's faithfulness. For this reason I ask you not to lose heart because of what I am suffering for you, which is your glory.

PRAYER FOR STRENGTHENED LOVE

For this reason I kneel before the Father, from whom every family in heaven and on earth is named. I pray that according to the wealth of his glory he will grant you to be strengthened with power through his Spirit in the inner person, that Christ will dwell in your hearts through faith, so that, because you have been rooted and grounded in love, you will be able to comprehend with all the saints what is the breadth and length and height and depth, and thus to know the love of Christ that surpasses knowledge, so that you will be filled up to all the fullness of God.

Now to him who by the power that is working within us is able to do far beyond all that we ask or think, to him be the glory in the church and in Christ Jesus to all generations, forever and ever. Amen.

CHAPTER 4

LIVE IN UNITY

I, therefore, the prisoner for the Lord, urge you to live worthily of the calling with which you have been called, with all humility and gentleness, with patience, putting up with one another in love, making every effort to keep the unity of the Spirit in the bond of peace. There is one body and one Spirit, just as you too were called to the one hope of your calling, one Lord, one faith, one baptism, one God and Father of all, who is over all and through all and in all.

But to each one of us grace was given according to the measure of Christ's gift. Therefore it says, *"When he ascended on high he captured captives; he gave gifts to men."* Now what is the meaning of *"he ascended,"* except that he also descended to the lower regions, namely, the earth? He, the very one who descended, is also the one who ascended above all the heavens, in order to fill all things. And he himself gave some as apostles, some as prophets, some as evangelists, and some as pastors and teachers, to equip the saints for the work of ministry, that is, to build up the body of Christ, until we all attain to the unity of the faith and of the knowledge of the Son of God—a mature person, attaining to the measure of Christ's full stature. So we are no longer to be children, tossed back and forth by waves and carried about by every wind of teaching by the trickery of people who craftily carry out their deceitful schemes. But practicing the truth in love, we will in all things grow up into Christ, who is the head. From him the whole body grows, fitted and held together through every supporting ligament. As each one does its part, the body builds itself up in love.

LIVE IN HOLINESS

So I say this, and insist in the Lord, that you no longer live as the Gentiles do, in the futility of their thinking. They are darkened in their understanding, being alienated from the life of God because of the ignorance that is in them due to the hardness of their hearts. Because they are callous, they have given themselves over to indecency for the practice of every kind of impurity with greediness. But you did not learn about Christ like this, if indeed you heard about him and were taught in him, just as the truth is in Jesus. You were taught with reference to your former way of life to lay aside the old man who is being corrupted in accordance with deceitful desires, to be renewed in the spirit of your mind, and to put on the new man who has been created in God's image—in righteousness and holiness that comes from truth.

Therefore, having laid aside falsehood, *each one of you speak the truth with his neighbor* because we are members of one another. *Be angry and do not sin;* do not let the sun go down on the cause of your anger. Do not give the devil an opportunity. The one who steals must steal no longer; instead he must labor, doing good with his own hands, so that he will have something to share with the one who has need. You must let no unwholesome word come out of your mouth, but only what is beneficial for the building up of the one in need, that it would give grace to those who hear. And do not grieve the Holy Spirit of God, by whom you were sealed for the day of redemption. You must put away all bitterness, anger, wrath, quarreling, and slanderous talk—indeed all malice. Instead, be kind to one another, compassionate, forgiving one another, just as God in Christ also forgave you.

CHAPTER 5

LIVE IN LOVE

Therefore, be imitators of God as dearly loved children and live in love, just as Christ also loved us and gave himself for us, a sacrificial and fragrant offering to God. But among you there must not be either sexual immorality, impurity of any kind, or greed, as these are not fitting for the saints. Neither should there be vulgar speech, foolish talk, or coarse jesting—all of which are out of character—but rather thanksgiving. For you can be confident of this one thing: that no person who is immoral, impure, or greedy (such a person is an idolater) has any inheritance in the kingdom of Christ and God.

LIVE IN THE LIGHT

Let nobody deceive you with empty words, for because of these things God's wrath comes on the sons of disobedience. Therefore do not be sharers with them, for you were at one time darkness, but now you are light in the Lord.

Live like children of light—for the fruit of the light consists in all goodness, righteousness, and truth—trying to learn what is pleasing to the Lord. Do not participate in the unfruitful deeds of darkness, but rather expose them. For the things they do in secret are shameful even to mention. But all things being exposed by the light are made visible. For everything made visible is light, and for this reason it says:

"Awake, O sleeper!
Rise from the dead,
and Christ will shine on you!"

LIVE WISELY

Therefore consider carefully how you live—not as unwise but as wise, taking advantage of every opportunity because the days are evil. For this reason do not be foolish, but be wise by understanding what the Lord's will is. And do not get drunk with wine, which is debauchery, but be filled by the Spirit, speaking to one another in psalms, hymns, and spiritual songs, singing and making music in your hearts to the Lord, always giving thanks to God the Father for all things in the name of our Lord Jesus Christ, and submitting to one another out of reverence for Christ.

EXHORTATIONS TO HOUSEHOLDS

Wives, submit to your husbands as to the Lord, because the husband is the head of the wife as also Christ is the head of the church (he himself being the savior of the body). But as the church submits to Christ, so also wives should submit to their husbands in everything. Husbands, love your wives just as Christ loved the church and gave himself for her to sanctify her by cleansing her with the washing of the water by the word, so that he may present the church to himself as glorious—not having a stain or wrinkle, or any such blemish, but holy and blameless. In the same way husbands ought to love their wives as their own bodies. He who loves his wife loves himself. For no one has ever hated his own body, but he feeds it and takes care of it, just as Christ also does the church, because we are members of his body. *For this reason a man will leave his father and mother and will be joined to his wife, and the two will become one flesh.* This mystery is great—but I am actually speaking with reference to Christ and the church. Nevertheless, each one of you must also love his own wife as he loves himself, and the wife must respect her husband.

CHAPTER 6

Children, obey your parents in the Lord, for this is right. *"Honor your father and mother,"* which is the first commandment accompanied by a promise, namely, *"that it will go well with you and that you will live a long time on the earth."*

Fathers, do not provoke your children to anger, but raise them up in the discipline and instruction of the Lord.

Slaves, obey your human masters with fear and trembling, in the sincerity of your heart, as to Christ, not like those who do their work only when someone is watching—as people-pleasers—but as slaves of Christ doing the will of God from the heart. Obey with enthusiasm, as though serving the Lord and not people, because you know that each person, whether slave or free, if he does something good, this will be rewarded by the Lord.

Masters, treat your slaves the same way, giving up the use of threats, because you know that both you and they have the same master in heaven, and there is no favoritism with him.

EXHORTATIONS FOR SPIRITUAL WARFARE

Finally, be strengthened in the Lord and in the strength of his power. Clothe yourselves with the full armor of God, so that you will be able to stand against the schemes of the devil. For our struggle is not against flesh and blood, but against the rulers, against the powers, against the world rulers of this darkness, against the spiritual forces of evil in the heavens. For this reason, take up the full armor of God so that you may be able to stand your ground on the evil day, and having done everything, to stand. Stand firm therefore, by fastening the belt of truth around your waist, by putting on the breastplate of righteousness, by fitting your feet with the preparation that comes from the good news of peace, and in all of this, by taking up the shield of faith with which you can extinguish all the flaming arrows of the evil one. And take *the helmet of salvation* and the sword of the Spirit (which is the word of God). With every prayer and petition, pray at all times in the Spirit, and to this end be alert, with all perseverance and petitions for all the saints. Pray for me also, that I may be given the right words when I begin to speak—that I may confidently make known the mystery of the gospel, for which I am an ambassador in chains. Pray that I may be able to speak boldly as I ought to speak.

FAREWELL COMMENTS

Tychicus, my dear brother and faithful servant in the Lord, will make everything known to you, so that you too may know about my circumstances, how I am doing. I have sent him to you for this very purpose, that you may know our circumstances and that he may encourage your hearts.

Peace to the brothers and sisters, and love with faith, from God the Father and the Lord Jesus Christ. Grace be with all those who love our Lord Jesus Christ with an undying love.

PHILIPPIANS

PROLOGUE

When the Philippians received a letter from Paul, they probably took a deep, nervous breath before beginning to read. They knew that Paul had written this letter from a prison cell. He had sacrificed beyond measure. He had been maligned, shipwrecked, beaten, stoned, and left for dead. He took stand after stand against false teachings. He invested time and teaching in other pastors and leaders. Through it all he had been faithful. Now he was in prison for the very thing Christ had called him to do. How would he respond? Would he feel that God had let him down? Would he be frustrated that the expansion of the gospel was now in jeopardy? Would he be discouraged? Hopeless? Angry?

Any of these responses would have been understandable. But as the Philippians began to read the letter, Paul's theme became quickly apparent. It was startling. It made no sense. Paul was responding to his adversity in a way that no one expected. And more than that, he invited the Philippians to react the same way.

CHAPTER 1

SALUTATION

From Paul and Timothy, slaves of Christ Jesus, to all the saints in Christ Jesus who are in Philippi, with the overseers and deacons. Grace and peace to you from God our Father and the Lord Jesus Christ!

PRAYER FOR THE CHURCH

I thank my God every time I remember you. I always pray with joy in my every prayer for all of you because of your participation in the gospel from the first day until now. For I am sure of this very thing, that the one who began a good work in you will perfect it until the day of Christ Jesus. For it is right for me to think this about all of you, because I have you in my heart, since both in my imprisonment and in the defense and confirmation of the gospel all of you became partners in God's grace together with me. For God is my witness that I long for all of you with the affection of Christ Jesus. And I pray this, that your love may abound even more and more in knowledge and every kind of insight so that you can decide what is best, and thus be sincere and blameless for the day of Christ, filled with the fruit of righteousness that comes through Jesus Christ to the glory and praise of God.

MINISTRY AS A PRISONER

I want you to know, brothers and sisters, that my situation has actually turned out to advance the gospel: The whole imperial guard and everyone else knows that I am in prison for the sake of Christ, and most of the brothers and sisters, having confidence in the Lord because of my imprisonment, now more than ever dare to speak the word fearlessly.

Some, to be sure, are preaching Christ from envy and rivalry, but others from goodwill. The latter do so from love because they know that I am placed here for the defense of the gospel. The former proclaim Christ from selfish ambition, not sincerely, because they think they can cause trouble for me in my imprisonment. What is the result? Only that in every way, whether in pretense or in truth, Christ is being proclaimed, and in this I rejoice.

Yes, and I will continue to rejoice, for I know that this will turn out for my deliverance through your prayers and the help of the Spirit of Jesus Christ. My confident hope is that I will in no way be ashamed but that with complete boldness, even now as always, Christ will be exalted in my body, whether I live or die. For to me, living is Christ and dying is gain. Now if I am to go on living in the body, this will mean productive work for me, yet I don't know which I prefer: I feel torn between the two because I have a desire to depart and be with Christ, which is better by far, but it is more vital for your sake that I remain in the body. And since I am sure of this, I know that I will remain and continue with all of you for the sake of your progress and joy in the faith, so that what you can be proud of may increase because of me in Christ Jesus, when I come back to you.

Only conduct yourselves in a manner worthy of the gospel of Christ so that—whether I come and see you or whether I remain absent—I should hear that you are standing firm in one spirit, with one mind, by contending side by side for the faith of the gospel, and by not being intimidated in any way by your opponents. This is a sign of their destruction, but of your salvation—a sign which is from God. For it has been granted to you not only to believe in Christ but also to suffer for him, since you are encountering the same conflict that you saw me face and now hear that I am facing.

CHAPTER 2

CHRISTIAN UNITY AND CHRIST'S HUMILITY

Therefore, if there is any encouragement in Christ, any comfort provided by love, any fellowship in the Spirit, any affection or mercy, complete my joy and be of the same mind, by having the same love, being united in spirit, and having one purpose. Instead of being motivated by selfish ambition or vanity, each of you should, in humility, be moved to treat one another as more important than yourself. Each of you should be concerned not only about your own interests, but about the interests of others as well. You should have

the same attitude toward one another that
Christ Jesus had,

> who, though he existed in the form of God,
> did not regard equality with God
> as something to be grasped,
> but emptied himself
> by taking on the form of a slave,
> by looking like other men,
> and by sharing in human nature.
> He humbled himself
> by becoming obedient to the point
>   of death
> —even death on a cross!
> As a result God highly exalted him
> and gave him the name
> that is above every name,
> so that at the name of Jesus
> every knee will bow
> —in heaven and on earth and under
>   the earth—
> and every tongue confess
> that Jesus Christ is Lord
> to the glory of God the Father.

LIGHTS IN THE WORLD

So then, my dear friends, just as you have
always obeyed, not only in my presence but
even more in my absence, continue working
out your salvation with awe and reverence,
for the one bringing forth in you both the desire and the effort—for the sake of his good
pleasure—is God. Do everything without

grumbling or arguing, so that you may be blameless and pure, children of God without blemish though you live in a crooked and perverse society, in which you shine as lights in the world by holding on to the word of life so that on the day of Christ I will have a reason to boast: that I did not run in vain nor labor in vain. But even if I am being poured out like a drink offering on the sacrifice and service of your faith, I am glad and rejoice together with all of you. And in the same way you also should be glad and rejoice together with me.

MODELS FOR MINISTRY

Now I hope in the Lord Jesus to send Timothy to you soon, so that I, too, may be encouraged by hearing news about you. For there is no one here like him who will readily demonstrate his deep concern for you. Others are busy with their own concerns, not those of Jesus Christ. But you know his qualifications that like a son working with his father, he served with me in advancing the gospel. So I hope to send him as soon as I know more about my situation, though I am confident in the Lord that I, too, will be coming to see you soon.

But for now I have considered it necessary to send Epaphroditus to you. For he is my brother, coworker and fellow soldier, and your messenger and minister to me in my need. Indeed, he greatly missed all of you and was distressed because you heard that he had been ill. In fact he became so ill that he nearly died. But God showed mercy to him—and not to him only, but also to me—so that I would not have grief on top of grief. Therefore I am all the more eager to send him, so that when you see him again you can rejoice and I can be free from anxiety. So welcome him in the Lord with great joy, and honor people like him, since it was because of the work of Christ that he almost died. He risked his life so that he could make up for your inability to serve me.

CHAPTER 3

TRUE AND FALSE RIGHTEOUSNESS

Finally, my brothers and sisters, rejoice in the Lord! To write this again is no trouble to me, and it is a safeguard for you.

Beware of the dogs, beware of the evil workers, beware of those who mutilate the flesh! For we are the circumcision, the ones who worship by the Spirit of God, exult in Christ Jesus, and do not rely on human credentials —though mine, too, are significant. If someone thinks he has good reasons to put confidence in human credentials, I have more: I was circumcised on the eighth day, from the people of Israel and the tribe of Benjamin, a Hebrew of Hebrews. I lived according to the law as a Pharisee. In my zeal for God I persecuted the church. According to the righteousness stipulated in the law I was blameless. But these assets I have come to regard as liabilities because of Christ. More than that, I now regard all things as liabilities compared to the far greater value of knowing Christ Jesus my Lord, for whom I have suffered the loss of all things—indeed, I regard them as dung!—that I may gain Christ and be found in him, not because I have my own righteousness derived from the law, but because I have the righteousness that comes by way of Christ's faithfulness—a righteousness from God that is in fact based on Christ's faithfulness. My aim is to know him, to experience the power of his resurrection, to share in his sufferings, and to be like him in his death, and so, somehow, to attain to the resurrection from the dead.

KEEP GOING FORWARD

Not that I have already attained this—that is, I have not already been perfected—but I strive to lay hold of that for which Christ Jesus also laid hold of me. Brothers and sisters, I do not consider myself to have attained this. Instead I am single-minded: Forgetting the things that are behind and reaching out for the things that are ahead, with this goal in mind, I strive toward the prize of the upward call of God in Christ Jesus. Therefore let those of us who are "perfect" embrace this point of view. If you think otherwise, God will reveal to you the error of your ways. Nevertheless, let us live up to the standard that we have already attained.

Be imitators of me, brothers and sisters, and watch carefully those who are living this way, just as you have us as an example. For many live, about whom I have often told you, and now, with tears, I tell you that they are the enemies of the cross of Christ. Their end is destruction, their god is the belly, they exult in their shame, and they think about earthly things. But our citizenship is in heaven—and we also eagerly await a savior from there, the Lord Jesus Christ, who will transform these humble bodies of ours into the likeness of his glorious body by means of that power by which he is able to subject all things to himself.

CHAPTER 4

CHRISTIAN PRACTICES

So then, my brothers and sisters, dear friends whom I long to see, my joy and crown, stand in the Lord in this way, my dear friends!

I appeal to Euodia and to Syntyche to agree in the Lord. Yes, I say also to you, true companion, help them. They have struggled together in the gospel ministry along with me and Clement and my other coworkers, whose names are in the book of life. Rejoice in the Lord always. Again I say, rejoice! Let everyone see your gentleness. The Lord is near! Do not be anxious about anything. Instead, in every situation, through prayer and petition with thanksgiving, tell your requests to God. And the peace of God that surpasses all understanding will guard your hearts and minds in Christ Jesus.

Finally, brothers and sisters, whatever is true, whatever is worthy of respect, whatever is just, whatever is pure, whatever is lovely, whatever is commendable, if something is excellent or praiseworthy, think about these things. And what you learned and received and heard and saw in me, do these things. And the God of peace will be with you.

APPRECIATION FOR SUPPORT

I have great joy in the Lord because now at last you have again expressed your concern for me. (Now I know you were concerned before but had no opportunity to do anything.) I am not saying this because I am in need, for I have learned to be content in any circumstance. I have experienced times of need and times of abundance. In any and every circumstance I have learned the secret of contentment, whether I go satisfied or hungry, have plenty or nothing. I am able to do all things through the one who strengthens me. Nevertheless, you did well to share with me in my trouble.

And as you Philippians know, at the beginning of my gospel ministry, when I left Macedonia, no church shared with me in this matter of giving and receiving except you alone. For even in Thessalonica on more than one occasion you sent something for my need. I do not say this because I am seeking a gift. Rather, I seek the credit that abounds to your account. For I have received everything, and I have plenty. I have all I need because I received from Epaphroditus what you sent—a fragrant offering, an acceptable sacrifice, very pleasing to God. And my God will supply your every need according to his glorious riches in Christ Jesus. May glory be given to God our Father forever and ever. Amen.

FINAL GREETINGS

Give greetings to all the saints in Christ Jesus. The brothers with me here send greetings. All the saints greet you, especially those who belong to Caesar's household. The grace of the Lord Jesus Christ be with your spirit.

COLOSSIANS

PROLOGUE

The Colossian believers lived in a city that was once prominent but now in decline. They were part of a church that Epaphras, a disciple of Paul's from Ephesus, had planted. It's likely the Colossians felt like second-class Christians who were part of a second-class church in a second-class city.

Paul, however, had quite a different opinion to give the Colossians. They overlooked one vital truth, the key to understanding their significance and worth rightly. It was the reason they could hold on to unwavering hope despite what was happening around them. What Paul wanted to remind the Colossians of—the one thing that could change their perspective on everything—found its power in its simplicity. It was time to remind the Colossians that their position aligned with the position of the one they followed.

CHAPTER 1

SALUTATION

From Paul, an apostle of Christ Jesus by the will of God, and Timothy our brother, to the saints, the faithful brothers and sisters in Christ, at Colossae. Grace and peace to you from God our Father!

PAUL'S THANKSGIVING AND PRAYER FOR THE CHURCH

We always give thanks to God, the Father of our Lord Jesus Christ, when we pray for you, since we heard about your faith in Christ Jesus and the love that you have for all the saints. Your faith and love have arisen from the hope laid up for you in heaven, which you have heard about in the message of truth, the gospel that has come to you. Just as in the entire world this gospel is bearing fruit and growing, so it has also been bearing fruit and growing among you from the first day you heard it and understood the grace of God in truth. You learned the gospel from Epaphras, our dear fellow slave—a faithful minister of Christ on our behalf—who also told us of your love in the Spirit.

PAUL'S PRAYER FOR THE GROWTH OF THE CHURCH

For this reason we also, from the day we heard about you, have not ceased praying for you and asking God to fill you with the knowledge of his will in all spiritual wisdom and understanding, so that you may live worthily

of the Lord and please him in all respects—
bearing fruit in every good deed, growing in
the knowledge of God, being strengthened
with all power according to his glorious might
for the display of all patience and steadfast-
ness, joyfully giving thanks to the Father who
has qualified you to share in the saints' inheritance in the light. He delivered us from
the power of darkness and transferred us to
the kingdom of the Son he loves, in whom we
have redemption, the forgiveness of sins.

THE SUPREMACY OF CHRIST

He is the image of the invisible God, the
firstborn over all creation,
for all things in heaven and on earth
were created in him—all things,
whether visible or invisible, whether
thrones or dominions, whether
principalities or powers—all things
were created through him and for him.
He himself is before all things, and all
things are held together in him.
He is the head of the body, the church,
as well as the beginning, the firstborn
from the dead, so that he himself may
become first in all things.
For God was pleased to have all his
fullness dwell in the Son
and through him to reconcile all things to
himself by making peace through the
blood of his cross—through him, whether
things on earth or things in heaven.

PAUL'S GOAL IN MINISTRY

And you were at one time strangers and enemies in your minds as expressed through your evil deeds, but now he has reconciled you by his physical body through death to present you holy, without blemish, and blameless before him—if indeed you remain in the faith, established and firm, without shifting from the hope of the gospel that you heard. This gospel has also been preached in all creation under heaven, and I, Paul, have become its servant.

Now I rejoice in my sufferings for you, and I fill up in my physical body—for the sake of his body, the church—what is lacking in the sufferings of Christ. I became a servant of the church according to the stewardship from God—given to me for you—in order to complete the word of God, that is, the mystery that has been kept hidden from ages and generations, but has now been revealed to his saints. God wanted to make known to them the glorious riches of this mystery among the Gentiles, which is Christ in you, the hope of glory. We proclaim him by instructing and teaching all people with all wisdom so that we may present every person mature in Christ. Toward this goal I also labor, struggling according to his power that powerfully works in me.

CHAPTER 2

For I want you to know how great a struggle I have for you, and for those in Laodicea, and for those who have not met me face to face. My goal is that their hearts, having been knit together in love, may be encouraged, and that they may have all the riches that assurance brings in their understanding of the knowledge of the mystery of God, namely, Christ, in whom are hidden all the treasures of wisdom and knowledge. I say this so that no one will deceive you through arguments that sound reasonable. For though I am absent from you in body, I am present with you in spirit, rejoicing to see your morale and the firmness of your faith in Christ.

WARNINGS AGAINST THE ADOPTION OF FALSE PHILOSOPHIES

Therefore, just as you received Christ Jesus as Lord, continue to live your lives in him, rooted and built up in him and firm in your faith just as you were taught, and overflowing with thankfulness. Be careful not to allow anyone to captivate you through an empty, deceitful philosophy that is according to human traditions and the elemental spirits of the world, and not according to Christ. For in him all the fullness of deity lives in bodily form, and you have been filled in him, who is the head over every ruler and authority. In him you also were circumcised—not, however, with a circumcision performed by human hands, but by the removal of the fleshly body, that is, through the circumcision done by Christ. Having been buried with him in baptism, you also have been raised with him through your faith in the power of God who raised him from the dead. And even though you were dead in your transgressions and in the uncircumcision of your flesh, he nevertheless made you alive with him, having forgiven all your transgressions. He has destroyed what was against us, a certificate of indebtedness expressed in decrees opposed to us. He has taken it away by nailing it to the cross. Disarming the rulers and authorities, he has made a public disgrace of them, triumphing over them by the cross.

Therefore do not let anyone judge you with respect to food or drink, or in the matter of a feast, new moon, or Sabbath days—these are only the shadow of the things to come, but the reality is Christ! Let no one who delights in false humility and the worship of angels pass judgment on you. That person goes on at great lengths about what he has supposedly seen, but he is puffed up with empty notions by his fleshly mind. He has not held fast to the head from whom the whole body, supported and knit together through its ligaments and sinews, grows with a growth that is from God.

If you have died with Christ to the elemental spirits of the world, why do you submit to them as though you lived in the world? "Do not handle! Do not taste! Do not touch!"

These are all destined to perish with use, founded as they are on human commands and teachings. Even though they have the appearance of wisdom with their self-imposed worship and humility achieved by an unsparing treatment of the body—a wisdom with no true value—they in reality result in fleshly indulgence.

CHAPTER 3

EXHORTATIONS TO SEEK THE THINGS ABOVE

Therefore, if you have been raised with Christ, keep seeking the things above, where Christ is, seated at the right hand of God. Keep thinking about things above, not things on the earth, for you have died and your life is hidden with Christ in God. When Christ (who is your life) appears, then you too will be revealed in glory with him. So put to death whatever in your nature belongs to the earth: sexual immorality, impurity, shameful passion, evil desire, and greed which is idolatry. Because of these things the wrath of God is coming on the sons of disobedience. You also lived your lives in this way at one time, when you used to live among them. But now, put off all such things as anger, rage, malice, slander, abusive language from your mouth. Do not lie to one another since you have put off the old man with its practices and have been clothed with the new man that is being renewed in knowledge according to the image of the one who created it. Here there is neither Greek nor Jew, circumcised or uncircumcised, barbarian, Scythian, slave or free, but Christ is all and in all.

EXHORTATION TO UNITY AND LOVE

Therefore, as the elect of God, holy and dearly loved, clothe yourselves with a heart of mercy, kindness, humility, gentleness, and patience, bearing with one another and forgiving one another, if someone happens to have a complaint against anyone else. Just as the Lord has forgiven you, so you also forgive others. And to all these virtues add love, which is the perfect bond. Let the peace of Christ be in control in your heart (for you were in fact called as one body to this peace), and be thankful. Let the word of Christ dwell in you richly, teaching and exhorting one another with all wisdom, singing psalms, hymns, and spiritual songs, all with grace in your hearts to God. And whatever you do in word or deed, do it all in the name of the Lord Jesus, giving thanks to God the Father through him.

EXHORTATION TO HOUSEHOLDS

Wives, submit to your husbands, as is fitting in the Lord. Husbands, love your wives and do not be embittered against them. Children, obey your parents in everything, for this is pleasing in the Lord. Fathers, do not provoke your children, so they will not become disheartened. Slaves, obey your earthly masters in every respect, not only when they are watching—like those who are strictly people-pleasers—but with a sincere heart, fearing the Lord. Whatever you are doing, work at it with enthusiasm, as to the Lord and not for people, because you know that you will receive your inheritance from the Lord as the reward. Serve the Lord Christ. For the one who does wrong will be repaid for his wrong, and there are no exceptions.

CHAPTER 4

Masters, treat your slaves with justice and fairness, because you know that you also have a master in heaven.

EXHORTATION TO PRAY FOR THE SUCCESS OF PAUL'S MISSION

Be devoted to prayer, keeping alert in it with thanksgiving. At the same time pray for us too, that God may open a door for the message so that we may proclaim the mystery of Christ, for which I am in chains. Pray that I may make it known as I should. Conduct yourselves with wisdom toward outsiders, making the most of the opportunities. Let your speech always be gracious, seasoned with salt, so that you may know how you should answer everyone.

PERSONAL GREETINGS AND INSTRUCTIONS

Tychicus, a dear brother, faithful minister, and fellow slave in the Lord, will tell you all the news about me. I sent him to you for this very purpose that you may know how we are doing and that he may encourage your hearts. I sent him with Onesimus, the faithful and dear brother, who is one of you. They will tell you about everything here.

Aristarchus, my fellow prisoner, sends you greetings, as does Mark, the cousin of Barnabas (about whom you received instructions; if he comes to you, welcome him). And Jesus who is called Justus also sends greetings. In terms of Jewish converts, these are the only fellow workers for the kingdom of God, and they have been a comfort to me. Epaphras, who is one of you and a slave of Christ, greets you. He is always struggling in prayer on your behalf, so that you may stand mature and fully assured in all the will of God. For I can testify that he has worked hard for you and for those in Laodicea and Hierapolis. Our dear friend Luke the physician and Demas greet you. Give my greetings to the brothers and sisters who are in Laodicea and to Nympha and the church that meets in her house. And after you have read this letter, have it read to the church of Laodicea. In turn, read the letter from Laodicea as well. And tell Archippus, "See to it that you complete the ministry you received in the Lord."

I, Paul, write this greeting by my own hand. Remember my chains. Grace be with you.

1 THESSALONIANS

PROLOGUE

The Thessalonian church knew what persecution looked like. The church had been recently born in the midst of adversity. Paul had preached for about a month with great success before opponents chased him out of the city, ending his ministry there. Although his visit had been short, Paul was concerned about the Thessalonian believers' well-being, so he sent Timothy from Corinth to check on them.

When Timothy returned to Corinth, he brought good news. The Thessalonian believers were well, standing firm even in the face of continuing oppression. The church did, however, have some questions, especially about "the day of the Lord." What was it and when would it happen?

It made sense that a church experiencing affliction would set its mind on Christ's return: on that day Jesus would make all things right. But the believers lacked a proper understanding of that glorious day. They needed to focus on the present as well as the future. Their situation was difficult, but they still had work to do.

CHAPTER 1

SALUTATION

From Paul and Silvanus and Timothy, to the church of the Thessalonians in God the Father and the Lord Jesus Christ. Grace and peace to you!

THANKSGIVING FOR RESPONSE TO THE GOSPEL

We thank God always for all of you as we mention you constantly in our prayers, because we recall in the presence of our God and Father your work of faith and labor of love and endurance of hope in our Lord Jesus Christ. We know, brothers and sisters loved by God, that he has chosen you, in that our gospel did not come to you merely in words, but in power and in the Holy Spirit and with deep conviction (surely you recall the character we displayed when we came among you to help you).

And you became imitators of us and of the Lord when you received the message with joy that comes from the Holy Spirit, despite great affliction. As a result you became an example to all the believers in Macedonia and in Achaia. For from you the message of the Lord has echoed forth not just in Macedonia and Achaia, but in every place reports of your faith in God have spread, so that we do not need to say anything. For people everywhere report how you welcomed us and how you turned to God from idols to serve the living and true God and to wait for his Son from heaven, whom he raised from the dead, Jesus our deliverer from the coming wrath.

CHAPTER 2

PAUL'S MINISTRY IN THESSALONICA

For you yourselves know, brothers and sisters, about our coming to you—it has not proven to be purposeless. But although we suffered earlier and were mistreated in Philippi, as you know, we had the courage in our God to declare to you the gospel of God in spite of much opposition. For the appeal we make does not come from error or impurity or with deceit, but just as we have been approved by God to be entrusted with the gospel, so we declare it, not to please people but God, who examines our hearts. For we never appeared with flattering speech, as you know, nor with a pretext for greed—God is our witness—nor to seek glory from people, either from you or from others, although we could have imposed our weight as apostles of Christ; instead we became little children among you. Like a nursing mother caring for her own children, with such affection for you we were happy to share with you not only the gospel of God but also our own lives, because you had become dear to us. For you recall, brothers and sisters, our toil and drudgery: By working night and day so as not to impose a burden on any of you, we preached to you the gospel of God. You are witnesses, and so is God, as to how holy and righteous and blameless our conduct was toward you who believe. As you know, we treated each one of you as a father treats his own children, exhorting and encouraging you and insisting that you live in a way worthy of God who calls you to his own kingdom and his glory. And so we too constantly thank God that when you received God's message that you heard from us, you accepted it not as a human message, but as it truly is, God's message, which is at work among you who believe. For you became imitators, brothers and sisters, of God's churches in Christ Jesus that are in Judea, because you too suffered the same things from your own countrymen as they in fact did from the Jews, who killed both the Lord Jesus and the prophets and persecuted us severely. They are displeasing to God and are opposed to all people because they hinder us from speaking to the Gentiles so that they may be saved. Thus they constantly fill up their measure of sins, but wrath has come upon them completely.

FORCED ABSENCE FROM THESSALONICA

But when we were separated from you, brothers and sisters, for a short time (in presence, not in affection) we became all the more fervent in our great desire to see you in person. For we wanted to come to you (I, Paul, in fact tried again and again), but Satan thwarted us. For who is our hope or joy or crown to boast of before our Lord Jesus at his coming? Is it not of course you? For you are our glory and joy!

CHAPTER 3

So when we could bear it no longer, we decided to stay on in Athens alone. We sent Timothy, our brother and fellow worker for God in the gospel of Christ, to strengthen you and encourage you about your faith, so that no one would be shaken by these afflictions. For you yourselves know that we are destined for this. For in fact when we were with you, we were telling you in advance that we would suffer affliction, and so it has happened, as you well know. So when I could bear it no longer, I sent to find out about your faith, for fear that the tempter somehow tempted you and our toil had proven useless.

But now Timothy has come to us from you and given us the good news of your faith and love and that you always think of us with affection and long to see us just as we also long to see you! So in all our distress and affliction, we were reassured about you, brothers and sisters, through your faith. For now we are alive again if you stand firm in the Lord. For how can we thank God enough for you, for all the joy we feel because of you before our God? We pray earnestly night and day to see you in person and make up what may be lacking in your faith.

Now may God our Father himself and our Lord Jesus direct our way to you. And may the Lord cause you to increase and abound in love for one another and for all, just as we do for you, so that your hearts are strengthened in holiness to be blameless before our God and Father at the coming of our Lord Jesus with all his saints.

CHAPTER 4

A LIFE PLEASING TO GOD

Finally then, brothers and sisters, we ask you and urge you in the Lord Jesus, that as you received instruction from us about how you must live and please God (as you are in fact living) that you do so more and more. For you know what commands we gave you through the Lord Jesus. For this is God's will: that you become holy, that you keep away from sexual immorality, that each of you know how to possess his own body in holiness and honor, not in lustful passion like the Gentiles who do not know God. In this matter no one should violate the rights of his brother or take advantage of him, because the Lord is the avenger in all these cases, as we also told you earlier and warned you solemnly. For God did not call us to impurity but in holiness. Consequently the one who rejects this is not rejecting human authority but God, who gives his Holy Spirit to you.

Now on the topic of brotherly love you have

no need for anyone to write you, for you yourselves are taught by God to love one another. And indeed you are practicing it toward all the brothers and sisters in all of Macedonia. But we urge you, brothers and sisters, to do so more and more, to aspire to lead a quiet life, to attend to your own business, and to work with your own hands, as we commanded you. In this way you will live a decent life before outsiders and not be in need.

THE LORD RETURNS FOR BELIEVERS

Now we do not want you to be uninformed, brothers and sisters, about those who are asleep, so that you will not grieve like the rest who have no hope. For if we believe that Jesus died and rose again, so also we believe that God will bring with him those who have fallen asleep as Christians. For we tell you this by the word of the Lord, that we who are alive, who are left until the coming of the Lord, will surely not go ahead of those who have fallen asleep. For the Lord himself will come down from heaven with a shout of command, with the voice of the archangel, and with the trumpet of God, and the dead in Christ will rise first. Then we who are alive, who are left, will be suddenly caught up together with them in the clouds to meet the Lord in the air. And so we will always be with the Lord. Therefore encourage one another with these words.

CHAPTER 5

THE DAY OF THE LORD

Now on the topic of times and seasons, brothers and sisters, you have no need for anything to be written to you. For you know quite well that the day of the Lord will come in the same way as a thief in the night. Now when they are saying, "There is peace and security," then sudden destruction comes on them, like labor pains on a pregnant woman, and they will surely not escape. But you, brothers and sisters, are not in the darkness for the day to overtake you like a thief would. For you all are sons of the light and sons of the day. We are not of the night nor of the darkness. So then we must not sleep as the rest, but must stay alert and sober. For those who sleep, sleep at night, and those who get drunk are drunk at night. But since we are of the day, we must stay sober *by putting on the breastplate* of faith and love and as *a helmet* our hope *for salvation*. For God did not destine us for wrath but for gaining salvation through our Lord Jesus Christ. He died for us so that whether we are alert or asleep, we will come to life together with him. Therefore encourage one another and build up each other, just as you are in fact doing.

FINAL INSTRUCTIONS

Now we ask you, brothers and sisters, to acknowledge those who labor among you and preside over you in the Lord and admonish you, and to esteem them most highly in love because of their work. Be at peace among yourselves. And we urge you, brothers and sisters, admonish the undisciplined, comfort the discouraged, help the weak, be patient toward all. See that no one pays back evil for evil to anyone, but always pursue what is good for one another and for all. Always rejoice, constantly pray, in everything give thanks. For this is God's will for you in Christ Jesus. Do not extinguish the Spirit. Do not treat prophecies with contempt. But examine all things; hold fast to what is good. Stay away from every form of evil.

CONCLUSION

Now may the God of peace himself make you completely holy and may your spirit and soul and body be kept entirely blameless at the coming of our Lord Jesus Christ. He who calls you is trustworthy, and he will in fact do this. Brothers and sisters, pray for us too. Greet all the brothers and sisters with a holy kiss. I call on you solemnly in the Lord to have this letter read to all the brothers and sisters. The grace of our Lord Jesus Christ be with you.

2 THESSALONIANS

PROLOGUE

In his first letter to the Thessalonians, Paul had called the believers to hold on to hope while waiting for Christ. But even in the short time since, Paul learned that some false teachings and misunderstandings about the end times had spread in the church, namely that the day of the Lord had already come. The Thessalonians feared they had missed Christ's return.

In response Paul wrote a follow-up letter correcting their mistakes about the day of the Lord. The Thessalonians could have confidence that the day of the Lord was yet to come, and when it did no one would miss it. The church had to continue to wait patiently with both hope and faithfulness.

CHAPTER 1

SALUTATION

From Paul and Silvanus and Timothy, to the church of the Thessalonians in God our

Father and the Lord Jesus Christ. Grace and peace to you from God the Father and the Lord Jesus Christ!

THANKSGIVING

We ought to thank God always for you, brothers and sisters, and rightly so, because your faith flourishes more and more and the love of each one of you all for one another is ever greater. As a result we ourselves boast about you in the churches of God for your perseverance and faith in all the persecutions and afflictions you are enduring.

ENCOURAGEMENT IN PERSECUTION

This is evidence of God's righteous judgment, to make you worthy of the kingdom of God, for which in fact you are suffering. For it is right for God to repay with affliction those who afflict you, and to you who are being afflicted to give rest together with us when the Lord Jesus is revealed from heaven with his mighty angels. *With flaming fire he will mete out punishment on those who do not know God* and do not obey the gospel of our Lord Jesus. They will undergo the penalty of eternal destruction, *away from the presence of the Lord and from the glory of his strength,* when he comes to be glorified among his saints and admired on that day among all who have believed—and you did in fact believe our testimony. And in this regard we pray for you always, that our God will make you worthy of his calling and fulfill by his power your every desire for goodness and every work of faith, that the name of our Lord Jesus may be glorified in you, and you in him, according to the grace of our God and the Lord Jesus Christ.

CHAPTER 2

THE DAY OF THE LORD

Now regarding the arrival of our Lord Jesus Christ and our being gathered to be with him, we ask you, brothers and sisters, not to be easily shaken from your composure or disturbed by any kind of spirit or message or letter allegedly from us, to the effect that the day of the Lord is already here. Let no one deceive you in any way. For that day will not arrive until the rebellion comes and the man of lawlessness is revealed, the son of destruction. He opposes *and exalts himself above every* so-called *god* or object of worship, and as a result *he takes his seat* in God's temple, displaying himself as God. Surely you recall that I used to tell you these things while I was still with you. And so you know what holds him back, so that he will be revealed in his own time. For the hidden power of lawlessness is already at work. However, the one who holds him back will do so until he is taken out of the way, and then the lawless one will be revealed, whom the Lord will destroy by the breath of his mouth and wipe out by the manifestation of his arrival. The arrival of the lawless one will be by Satan's working with all kinds of miracles and signs and false wonders, and with every kind of evil deception directed against those who are perishing, because they found no place in their hearts for the truth so as to be saved. Consequently God sends on them a deluding influence so that they will believe what is false. And so all of them who have not believed the truth but have delighted in evil will be condemned.

CALL TO STAND FIRM

But we ought to thank God always for you, brothers and sisters loved by the Lord, because God chose you from the beginning for salvation through sanctification by the Spirit and faith in the truth. He called you to this salvation through our gospel, so that you may possess the glory of our Lord Jesus Christ. Therefore, brothers and sisters, stand firm and hold on to the traditions that we taught you, whether by speech or by letter. Now may our Lord Jesus Christ himself and God our Father, who loved us and by grace gave us eternal comfort and good hope, encourage your hearts and strengthen you in every good thing you do or say.

CHAPTER 3

REQUEST FOR PRAYER

Finally, pray for us, brothers and sisters, that the Lord's message may spread quickly and be honored as in fact it was among you, and that we may be delivered from perverse and evil people. For not all have faith. But the Lord is faithful, and he will strengthen you and protect you from the evil one. And we are confident about you in the Lord that you are both doing—and will do—what we are commanding. Now may the Lord direct your hearts toward the love of God and the endurance of Christ.

RESPONSE TO THE UNDISCIPLINED

But we command you, brothers and sisters, in the name of our Lord Jesus Christ, to keep away from any brother who lives an undisciplined life and not according to the tradition they received from us. For you know yourselves how you must imitate us, because we did not behave without discipline among you, and we did not eat anyone's food without paying. Instead, in toil and drudgery we worked night and day in order not to burden any of you. It was not because we do not have that right, but to give ourselves as an example for you to imitate. For even when we were with you, we used to give you this command: "If anyone is not willing to work, neither should he eat." For we hear that some among you are living an undisciplined life, not doing their own work but meddling in the work of others. Now such people we command and urge in the Lord Jesus Christ to work quietly and so provide their own food to eat. But you, brothers and sisters, do not grow weary in doing what is right. But if anyone does not obey our message through this letter, take note of him and do not associate closely with him, so that he may be ashamed. Yet do not regard him as an enemy, but admonish him as a brother.

CONCLUSION

Now may the Lord of peace himself give you peace at all times and in every way. The Lord be with you all. I, Paul, write this greeting with my own hand, which is how I write in every letter. The grace of our Lord Jesus Christ be with you all.

1 TIMOTHY

PROLOGUE

Being young can be difficult. Being a young leader in a church brings an extra set of challenges. Ever since Timothy had joined Paul's second missionary journey, the apostle had apprenticed the younger man and even considered him a "genuine child in the faith." Paul had taught Timothy much, but he was not done mentoring him yet.

Timothy was now serving the Ephesus church, and Paul wanted to make sure that he had a vivid picture of what a Christ-honoring congregation looked like. Drawing from his experience and authority as an apostle, Paul wrote a letter to his protégé outlining the key marks of a healthy church. Each church would be different because of its location and members. But Paul had in mind certain nonessentials that must be present in any church. Timothy needed to be sure that his church followed the plan Paul was about to give him.

CHAPTER 1

SALUTATION

From Paul, an apostle of Christ Jesus by the command of God our Savior and of Christ Jesus our hope, to Timothy, my genuine child in the faith. Grace, mercy, and peace from God the Father and Christ Jesus our Lord!

TIMOTHY'S TASK IN EPHESUS

As I urged you when I was leaving for Macedonia, stay on in Ephesus to instruct certain people not to spread false teachings, nor to occupy themselves with myths and interminable genealogies. Such things promote useless speculations rather than God's redemptive plan that operates by faith. But the aim of our instruction is love that comes from a pure heart, a good conscience, and a sincere faith. Some have strayed from these and turned away to empty discussion. They want to be teachers of the law, but they do not understand what they are saying or the things they insist on so confidently.

But we know that the law is good if someone uses it legitimately, realizing that law is not intended for a righteous person, but for lawless and rebellious people, for the ungodly and sinners, for the unholy and profane, for those who kill their fathers or mothers, for murderers, sexually immoral people, practicing homosexuals, kidnappers, liars, perjurers—in fact, for any who live contrary to sound teaching. This accords with the glorious gospel of the blessed God that was entrusted to me.

I am grateful to the one who has strengthened me, Christ Jesus our Lord, because he considered me faithful in putting me into ministry, even though I was formerly a blasphemer and a persecutor, and an arrogant man. But I was treated with mercy because I acted ignorantly in unbelief, and our Lord's grace was abundant, bringing faith and love in Christ Jesus. This saying is trustworthy and deserves full acceptance: "Christ Jesus came into the world to save sinners"—and I am the worst of them! But here is why I was treated with mercy: so that in me as the worst, Christ Jesus could demonstrate his utmost patience, as an example for those who are going to believe in him for eternal life. Now to the eternal King, immortal, invisible, the only God, be honor and glory forever and ever! Amen.

I put this charge before you, Timothy my child, in keeping with the prophecies once spoken about you, in order that with such encouragement you may fight the good fight. To do this you must hold firmly to faith and a good conscience, which some have rejected and so have suffered shipwreck in regard to the faith. Among these are Hymenaeus and Alexander, whom I handed over to Satan to be taught not to blaspheme.

CHAPTER 2

PRAYER FOR ALL PEOPLE

First of all, then, I urge that requests, prayers, intercessions, and thanks be offered on behalf of all people, even for kings and all who are in authority, that we may lead a peaceful and quiet life in all godliness and dignity. Such prayer for all is good and welcomed before God our Savior, since he wants all people to be saved and to come to a knowledge of the truth. For there is one God and one intermediary between God and humanity, Christ Jesus, himself human, who gave himself as a ransom for all, revealing God's purpose at his appointed time. For this I was appointed a preacher and apostle—I am telling the truth; I am not lying—and a teacher of the Gentiles in faith and truth. So I want the men in every place to pray, lifting up holy hands without anger or dispute.

CONDUCT OF WOMEN

Likewise the women are to dress in suitable apparel, with modesty and self-control. Their adornment must not be with braided hair and gold or pearls or expensive clothing, but with good deeds, as is proper for women who profess reverence for God. A woman must learn quietly with all submissiveness. But I do not allow a woman to teach or exercise authority over a man. She must remain quiet. For Adam was formed first and then Eve. And

Adam was not deceived, but the woman, because she was fully deceived, fell into transgression. But she will be delivered through childbearing, if she continues in faith and love and holiness with self-control.

CHAPTER 3

QUALIFICATIONS FOR OVERSEERS AND DEACONS

This saying is trustworthy: "If someone aspires to the office of overseer, he desires a good work." The overseer then must be above reproach, the husband of one wife, temperate, self-controlled, respectable, hospitable, an able teacher, not a drunkard, not violent, but gentle, not contentious, free from the love of money. He must manage his own household well and keep his children in control without losing his dignity. But if someone does not know how to manage his own household, how will he care for the church of God? He must not be a recent convert, or he may become arrogant and fall into the punishment that the devil will exact. And he must be well thought of by those outside the faith, so that he may not fall into disgrace and be caught by the devil's trap.

Deacons likewise must be dignified, not two-faced, not given to excessive drinking, not greedy for gain, holding to the mystery of the faith with a clear conscience. And these also must be tested first and then let them serve as deacons if they are found blameless. Likewise also their wives must be dignified, not slanderous, temperate, faithful in every respect. Deacons must be husbands of one wife and good managers of their children and their own households. For those who have served well as deacons gain a good standing for themselves and great boldness in the faith that is in Christ Jesus.

CONDUCT IN GOD'S CHURCH

I hope to come to you soon, but I am writing these instructions to you in case I am delayed to let you know how people ought to conduct themselves in the household of God, because it is the church of the living God, the support and bulwark of the truth. And we all agree, our religion contains amazing revelation:

He was revealed in the flesh,
vindicated by the Spirit,
seen by angels,
proclaimed among Gentiles,
believed on in the world,
taken up in glory.

CHAPTER 4

TIMOTHY'S MINISTRY IN THE LATER TIMES

Now the Spirit explicitly says that in the later times some will desert the faith and occupy themselves with deceiving spirits and demonic teachings, influenced by the hypocrisy of liars whose consciences are seared. They will prohibit marriage and require abstinence from foods that God created to be received with thanksgiving by those who believe and know the truth. For every creation of God is good, and no food is to be rejected if it is received with thanksgiving. For it is sanctified by God's word and by prayer.

By pointing out such things to the brothers and sisters, you will be a good servant of Christ Jesus, having nourished yourself on the words of the faith and of the good teaching that you have followed. But reject those myths fit only for the godless and gullible, and train yourself for godliness. For "physical exercise has some value, but godliness is valuable in every way. It holds promise for the present life and for the life to come." This saying is trustworthy and deserves full acceptance. In fact this is why we work hard and struggle, because we have set our hope on the living God, who is the Savior of all people, especially of believers.

Command and teach these things. Let no one look down on you because you are young, but set an example for the believers in your speech, conduct, love, faithfulness, and purity. Until I come, give attention to the public reading of scripture, to exhortation, to teaching. Do not neglect the spiritual gift you have, given to you and confirmed by prophetic words when the elders laid hands on you. Take pains with these things; be absorbed in them, so that everyone will see your progress. Be conscientious about how you live and what you teach. Persevere in this, because by doing so you will save both yourself and those who listen to you.

CHAPTER 5

INSTRUCTIONS ABOUT SPECIFIC GROUPS

Do not address an older man harshly but appeal to him as a father. Speak to younger men as brothers, older women as mothers, and younger women as sisters—with complete purity.

Honor widows who are truly in need. But if a widow has children or grandchildren, they should first learn to fulfill their duty toward their own household and so repay their parents what is owed them. For this is what pleases God. But the widow who is truly in need, and completely on her own, has set her hope on God and continues in her pleas and prayers night and day. But the one who lives for pleasure is dead even while she lives. Reinforce these commands, so that they will be beyond reproach. But if someone does not provide for his own, especially his own family, he has denied the faith and is worse than an unbeliever.

No widow should be put on the list unless she is at least sixty years old, was the wife of one husband, and has a reputation for good works: as one who has raised children, practiced hospitality, washed the feet of the saints, helped those in distress—as one who has exhibited all kinds of good works. But do not accept younger widows on the list, because their passions may lead them away from Christ and they will desire to marry, and so incur judgment for breaking their former pledge. And besides that, going around from house to house they learn to be lazy, and they are not only lazy, but also gossips and busybodies, talking about things they should not. So I want younger women to marry, raise children, and manage a household, in order to give the adversary no opportunity to vilify us. For some have already wandered away to follow Satan. If a believing woman has widows in her family, let her help them. The church should not be burdened so that it may help the widows who are truly in need.

Elders who provide effective leadership must be counted worthy of double honor, especially those who work hard in speaking and teaching. For the scripture says, "*Do not muzzle an ox while it is treading out the grain*," and, "The worker deserves his pay." Do not accept an accusation against an elder unless it can be confirmed *by two or three witnesses.* Those guilty of sin must be rebuked before all, as a warning to the rest. Before God and Christ Jesus and the elect angels, I solemnly charge you to carry out these commands without prejudice or favoritism of any kind. Do not lay hands on anyone hastily and so identify with the sins of others. Keep yourself pure. (Stop drinking just water, but use a little wine for your digestion and your frequent illnesses.) The sins of some people are obvious, going before them into judgment, but for others, they show up later. Similarly good works are also obvious, and the ones that are not cannot remain hidden.

CHAPTER 6

Those who are under the yoke as slaves must regard their own masters as deserving of full respect. This will prevent the name of God and Christian teaching from being discredited. But those who have believing masters must not show them less respect because they are brothers. Instead they are to serve all the more, because those who benefit from their service are believers and dearly loved.

SUMMARY OF TIMOTHY'S DUTIES

Teach them and exhort them about these things. If someone spreads false teachings and does not agree with sound words (that is, those of our Lord Jesus Christ) and with the teaching that accords with godliness, he is conceited and understands nothing, but has an unhealthy interest in controversies and verbal disputes. This gives rise to envy, dissension, slanders, evil suspicions, and constant bickering by people corrupted in their minds and deprived of the truth, who suppose that godliness is a way of making a profit. Now godliness combined with contentment brings great profit. For we have brought nothing into this world and so we cannot take a single thing out either. But if we have food and shelter, we will be satisfied with that. Those who long to be rich, however, stumble into temptation and a trap and many senseless and harmful desires that plunge people into ruin and destruction. For the love of money is the root of all evils. Some people in reaching for it have strayed from the faith and stabbed themselves with many pains.

But you, as a person dedicated to God, keep away from all that. Instead pursue righteousness, godliness, faithfulness, love, endurance, and gentleness. Compete well for the faith and lay hold of that eternal life you were called for and made your good confession for in the presence of many witnesses. I charge you before God who gives life to all things and Christ Jesus who made his good confession before Pontius Pilate, to obey this command without fault or failure until the appearing of our Lord Jesus Christ —whose appearing the blessed and only Sovereign, the King of kings and Lord of lords, will reveal at the right time. He alone possesses immortality and lives in unapproachable light, whom no human has ever seen or is able to see. To him be honor and eternal power! Amen.

Command those who are rich in this world's goods not to be haughty or to set their hope on riches, which are uncertain, but on God who richly provides us with all things for our enjoyment. Tell them to do good, to be rich in good deeds, to be generous givers, sharing with others. In this way they will save up a treasure for themselves as a firm foundation for the future and so lay hold of what is truly life.

CONCLUSION

O Timothy, protect what has been entrusted to you. Avoid the profane chatter and absurdities of so-called "knowledge." By professing it, some have strayed from the faith. Grace be with you all.

2 TIMOTHY

PROLOGUE

Paul knew that this letter to Timothy might be his last. Several years had passed since the apostle had written to the young man outlining what a healthy church should look like. Paul wrote that letter just after his release from prison, but now he was jailed once more. This time, however, it didn't look as though he would be leaving.

What should he say to Timothy, his fellow worker, longtime friend, and son in the faith? Paul's life was nearly at its end, but Timothy, God willing, still had many years in front of him. The young man had so many opportunities to serve Christ and his church. What parting words would resonate most with him? What teachings could Timothy hold on to and return to as he grew in his faith and in his leadership role? How could Paul best prepare his friend for long-term ministry?

As Paul began to write, his heart for Timothy affected each word he wrote. Paul had previously emphasized how critical it was for the church to be managed by godly leaders. Now he would remind Timothy of that in the most personal way.

CHAPTER 1

SALUTATION

From Paul, an apostle of Christ Jesus by the will of God, to further the promise of life in Christ Jesus, to Timothy, my dear child. Grace, mercy, and peace from God the Father and Christ Jesus our Lord!

THANKSGIVING AND CHARGE TO TIMOTHY

I am thankful to God, whom I have served with a clear conscience as my ancestors did, when I remember you in my prayers as I do constantly night and day. As I remember your tears, I long to see you, so that I may be filled with joy. I recall your sincere faith that was alive first in your grandmother Lois and in your mother Eunice, and I am sure is in you.

Because of this I remind you to rekindle God's gift that you possess through the laying on of my hands. For God did not give us a Spirit of fear but of power and love and self-control. So do not be ashamed of the testimony about our Lord or of me, a prisoner for his sake, but by God's power accept your share of suffering for the gospel. He is the one who saved us and called us with a holy calling, not based on our works but on his own purpose and grace, granted to us in Christ Jesus before time began, but now made visible through the appearing of our Savior Christ Jesus. He has broken the power of death and brought life and immortality to light through the gospel! For this gospel I was appointed a preacher and apostle and teacher. Because of this, in fact, I suffer as I do. But I am not ashamed because I know the one in whom my faith is set and I am convinced that he is able to protect what has been entrusted to me until that day. Hold to the standard of sound words that you heard from me and do so with the faith and love that are in Christ Jesus. Protect that good thing entrusted to you, through the Holy Spirit who lives within us.

You know that everyone in the province of Asia deserted me, including Phygelus and Hermogenes. May the Lord grant mercy to the family of Onesiphorus because he often refreshed me and was not ashamed of my imprisonment. But when he arrived in Rome, he eagerly searched for me and found me. May the Lord grant him to find mercy from the Lord on that day! And you know very well all the ways he served me in Ephesus.

CHAPTER 2

SERVING FAITHFULLY DESPITE HARDSHIP

So you, my child, be strong in the grace that is in Christ Jesus. And what you heard me say in the presence of many witnesses entrust to faithful people who will be competent to teach others as well. Take your share of suffering as a good soldier of Christ Jesus. No one in military service gets entangled in matters of everyday life; otherwise he will not please the one who recruited him. Also, if anyone competes as an athlete, he will not be crowned as the winner unless he competes according to the rules. The farmer who works hard ought to have the first share of the crops. Think about what I am saying and the Lord will give you understanding of all this.

Remember Jesus Christ, raised from the dead, a descendant of David; such is my gospel, for which I suffer hardship to the point of imprisonment as a criminal, but God's message is not imprisoned! So I endure all things for the sake of those chosen by God, that they, too, may obtain salvation in Christ Jesus and its eternal glory. This saying is trustworthy:

If we died with him, we will also live with him.

If we endure, we will also reign with him.

If we deny him, he will also deny us.

If we are unfaithful, he remains faithful, since he cannot deny himself.

DEALING WITH FALSE TEACHERS

Remind people of these things and solemnly charge them before the Lord not to wrangle over words. This is of no benefit; it just brings ruin on those who listen. Make every effort to present yourself before God as a proven worker who does not need to be ashamed, teaching the message of truth accurately. But avoid profane chatter because those occupied with it will stray further and further into ungodliness, and their message will spread its infection like gangrene. Hymenaeus and Philetus are in this group. They have strayed from the truth by saying that the resurrection has already occurred, and they are undermining some people's faith. However, God's solid foundation remains standing, bearing this seal: *"The Lord knows those who are his,"* and "Everyone who confesses the name of the Lord must turn away from evil."

Now in a wealthy home there are not only gold and silver vessels, but also ones made of wood and of clay, and some are for honorable use, but others for ignoble use. So if someone cleanses himself of such behavior, he will be a vessel for honorable use, set apart, useful for the Master, prepared for every good work. But keep away from youthful passions, and pursue righteousness, faithfulness, love, and peace, in company with others who call on the Lord from a pure heart. But reject foolish and ignorant controversies because you know they breed infighting. And the Lord's slave must not engage in heated disputes but be kind toward all, an apt teacher, patient, correcting opponents with gentleness. Perhaps God will grant them repentance and then knowledge of the truth, and they will come to their senses and escape the devil's trap where they are held captive to do his will.

CHAPTER 3

MINISTRY IN THE LAST DAYS

But understand this, that in the last days difficult times will come. For people will be lovers of themselves, lovers of money, boastful, arrogant, blasphemers, disobedient to parents, ungrateful, unholy, unloving, irreconcilable, slanderers, without self-control, savage, opposed to what is good, treacherous, reckless, conceited, loving pleasure rather than loving God. They will maintain the outward appearance of religion but will have repudiated its power. So avoid people like these. For some of these insinuate themselves into households and captivate weak women who are overwhelmed with sins and led along by various passions. Such women are always seeking instruction, yet never able to arrive at a knowledge of the truth. And just as Jannes and Jambres opposed Moses, so these people—who have warped minds and are disqualified in the faith—also oppose the truth. But they will not go much further, for their foolishness will be obvious to everyone, just like it was with Jannes and Jambres.

CONTINUE IN WHAT YOU HAVE LEARNED

You, however, have followed my teaching, my way of life, my purpose, my faith, my patience, my love, my endurance, as well as the persecutions and sufferings that happened to me in Antioch, in Iconium, and in Lystra. I endured these persecutions, and the Lord delivered me from them all. Now in fact all who want to live godly lives in Christ Jesus will be persecuted. But evil people and charlatans will go from bad to worse, deceiving others and being deceived themselves. You, however, must continue in the things you have learned and are confident about. You know who taught you and how from infancy you have known the holy writings, which are able to give you wisdom for salvation through faith in Christ Jesus. Every scripture is inspired by God and useful for teaching, for reproof, for correction, and for training in righteousness, that the person dedicated to God may be capable and equipped for every good work.

CHAPTER 4

CHARGE TO TIMOTHY REPEATED

I solemnly charge you before God and Christ Jesus, who is going to judge the living and the dead, and by his appearing and his kingdom: Preach the message, be ready whether it is convenient or not, reprove, rebuke, exhort with complete patience and instruction. For there will be a time when people will not tolerate sound teaching. Instead, following their own desires, they will accumulate teachers for themselves because they have an insatiable curiosity to hear new things. And they will turn away from hearing the truth, but on the other hand they will turn aside to myths. You, however, be self-controlled in all things, endure hardship, do an evangelist's work, fulfill your ministry. For I am already being poured out as an offering, and the time for me to depart is at hand. I have competed well; I have finished the race; I have kept the faith! Finally the crown of righteousness is reserved for me. The Lord, the righteous Judge, will award it to me in that day—and not to me only, but also to all who have set their affection on his appearing.

TRAVEL PLANS AND CONCLUDING GREETINGS

Make every effort to come to me soon. For Demas deserted me, since he loved the present age, and he went to Thessalonica. Crescens went to Galatia and Titus to Dalmatia. Only Luke is with me. Get Mark and bring him with you because he is a great help to me in ministry. Now I have sent Tychicus to Ephesus. When you come, bring with you the cloak I left in Troas with Carpas and the scrolls, especially the parchments. Alexander the coppersmith did me a great deal of harm. *The Lord will repay him in keeping with his deeds.* You be on guard against him too, because he vehemently opposed our words. At my first defense no one appeared in my support; instead they all deserted me—may they not be held accountable for it. But the Lord stood by me and strengthened me, so that through me the message would be fully proclaimed for all the Gentiles to hear. And so I was delivered from the lion's mouth! The Lord will deliver me from every evil deed and will bring me safely into his heavenly kingdom. To him be glory for ever and ever! Amen.

Greetings to Prisca and Aquila and the family of Onesiphorus. Erastus stayed in Corinth. Trophimus I left ill in Miletus. Make every effort to come before winter. Greetings to you from Eubulus, Pudens, Linus, Claudia, and all the brothers and sisters. The Lord be with your spirit. Grace be with you.

TITUS

PROLOGUE

Titus became a follower of Christ because of Paul. But the apostle did not stop there. He took Titus under his wing and in time Titus became one of his most reliable ministry partners. The two frequently traveled together and Paul mentioned his protégé in several letters.

Eventually, Titus would serve the church on the island of Crete, an important commercial center in the Mediterranean Sea. Prosperity, however, brought bad habits for the Cretans, who had developed a reputation for being dishonest and lazy. Even worse, aspects of these characteristics had seeped into the church. When Paul heard that some of the believers on Crete were acting selfishly, he knew that he had to get it corrected.

Paul wrote to warn his friend that the church needed to stand out from the culture around it. The people of Crete may have valued being idle, but the church should be marked by work. Here Paul didn't have vocation in mind, though that was important. Jesus had given the church a different job—a most vital job—to do.

CHAPTER 1

SALUTATION

From Paul, a slave of God and apostle of Jesus Christ, to further the faith of God's chosen ones and the knowledge of the truth that is in keeping with godliness, in hope of eternal life, which God, who does not lie, promised before time began. But now in his own time he has made his message evident through the preaching I was entrusted with according to the command of God our Savior. To Titus, my genuine son in a common faith. Grace and peace from God the Father and Christ Jesus our Savior!

TITUS' TASK ON CRETE

The reason I left you in Crete was to set in order the remaining matters and to appoint elders in every town, as I directed you. An elder must be blameless, the husband of one wife, with faithful children who cannot be charged with dissipation or rebellion. For the overseer must be blameless as one entrusted with God's work, not arrogant, not prone to anger, not a drunkard, not violent, not greedy for gain. Instead he must be hospitable, devoted to what is good, sensible, upright, devout, and self-controlled. He must hold firmly to the faithful message as it has been taught, so that he will be able to give exhortation in such healthy teaching and correct those who speak against it.

For there are many rebellious people, idle talkers, and deceivers, especially those with Jewish connections, who must be silenced because they mislead whole families by teaching for dishonest gain what ought not to be taught. A certain one of them, in fact, one of their own prophets, said, "Cretans are always liars, evil beasts, lazy gluttons." Such testimony is true. For this reason rebuke them sharply that they may be healthy in the faith and not pay attention to Jewish myths and commands of people who reject the truth. All is pure to those who are pure. But to those who are corrupt and unbelieving, nothing is pure, but both their minds and consciences are corrupted. They profess to know God but with their deeds they deny him, since they are detestable, disobedient, and unfit for any good deed.

CHAPTER 2

CONDUCT CONSISTENT WITH SOUND TEACHING

But as for you, communicate the behavior that goes with sound teaching. Older men are to be temperate, dignified, self-controlled, sound in faith, in love, and in endurance. Older women likewise are to exhibit behavior fitting for those who are holy, not slandering, not slaves to excessive drinking, but teaching what is good. In this way they will train the younger women to love their husbands, to love their children, to be self-controlled, pure, fulfilling their duties at home, kind, being subject to their own husbands, so that the message of God may not be discredited. Encourage younger men likewise to be self-controlled, showing yourself to be an example of good works in every way. In your teaching show integrity, dignity, and a sound message that cannot be criticized, so that any opponent will be at a loss because he has nothing evil to say about us. Slaves are to be subject to their own masters in everything, to do what is wanted and not talk back, not pilfering, but showing all good faith, in order to bring credit to the teaching of God our Savior in everything.

For the grace of God has appeared, bringing salvation to all people. It trains us to reject godless ways and worldly desires and to live self-controlled, upright, and godly lives in the present age, as we wait for the happy fulfillment of our hope in the glorious appearing of our great God and Savior, Jesus Christ. He gave himself for us to set us free from every kind of lawlessness and to purify for himself a people who are truly his, who are eager to do good. So communicate these things with the sort of exhortation or rebuke that carries full authority. Don't let anyone look down on you.

CHAPTER 3

CONDUCT TOWARD THOSE OUTSIDE THE CHURCH

Remind them to be subject to rulers and authorities, to be obedient, to be ready for every good work. They must not slander anyone, but be peaceable, gentle, showing complete courtesy to all people. For we, too, were once foolish, disobedient, misled, enslaved to various passions and desires, spending our lives in evil and envy, hateful and hating one another. But "when the kindness of God our Savior and his love for mankind appeared, he saved us not by works of righteousness that we have done but on the basis of his mercy, through the washing of the new birth and the renewing of the Holy Spirit, whom he poured out on us in full measure through Jesus Christ our Savior. And so, since we have been justified by his grace, we become heirs with the confident expectation of eternal life."

SUMMARY OF THE LETTER

This saying is trustworthy, and I want you to insist on such truths, so that those who have placed their faith in God may be intent on engaging in good works. These things are good and beneficial for all people. But avoid foolish controversies, genealogies, quarrels, and fights about the law because they are useless and empty. Reject a divisive person after one or two warnings. You know that such a person is twisted by sin and is conscious of it himself.

FINAL INSTRUCTIONS AND GREETING

When I send Artemas or Tychicus to you, do your best to come to me at Nicopolis, for I have decided to spend the winter there. Make every effort to help Zenas the lawyer and Apollos on their way; make sure they have what they need. Here is another way that our people can learn to engage in good works to meet pressing needs and so not be unfruitful. Everyone with me greets you. Greet those who love us in the faith. Grace be with you all.

PHILEMON

PROLOGUE

Onesimus had been a slave in Philemon's household until one day he decided to flee. He made his way to Rome, where he met Paul and became a fellow believer in Christ. Paul found Onesimus to be quite helpful, so he sort of wanted the former slave to stay in Rome. But he also recognized that the way Onesimus had left Philemon's household probably caused conflict. If Philemon harbored any bitterness toward Onesimus for what he had done, that would be a problem. Onesimus was now a believer. Any rift in the church was a problem. Paul had to try to repair this relationship.

Paul's plan was to send Onesimus back to Philemon. But he would not send him empty-handed. Paul first wrote a letter to Philemon and gave it to Onesimus to deliver. He could have chosen to use his authority as an apostle to tell Philemon what to do, but there was a better way. He wanted Philemon to *want* to reconcile with Onesimus.

The key for Paul was helping Philemon to see the situation the right way. Yes, Onesimus may have caused an issue in the way he left, but now a different man—a new man—was returning and would face Philemon with a letter in hand. And in that moment, Philemon had a choice to make.

CHAPTER 1

SALUTATION

From Paul, a prisoner of Christ Jesus, and Timothy our brother, to Philemon, our dear friend and colaborer, to Apphia our sister, to Archippus our fellow soldier, and to the church that meets in your house. Grace and peace to you from God our Father and the Lord Jesus Christ!

THANKS FOR PHILEMON'S LOVE AND FAITH

I always thank my God as I remember you in my prayers, because I hear of your faith in the Lord Jesus and your love for all the saints. I pray that the faith you share with us may deepen your understanding of every blessing that belongs to you in Christ. I have had great joy and encouragement because of your love, for the hearts of the saints have been refreshed through you, brother.

PAUL'S REQUEST FOR ONESIMUS

So, although I have quite a lot of confidence in Christ and could command you to do what is proper, I would rather appeal to you on the basis of love—I, Paul, an old man and even now a prisoner for the sake of Christ Jesus—I am appealing to you concerning my child, whose spiritual father I have become during my imprisonment, that is, Onesimus, who was formerly useless to you, but is now useful to you and me. I have sent him (who is my very heart) back to you. I wanted to keep him with me so that he could serve me in your place during my imprisonment for the sake of the gospel. However, without your consent I did not want to do anything so that your good deed would not be out of compulsion, but from your own willingness. For perhaps it was for this reason that he was separated from you for a little while so that you would have him back eternally, no longer as a slave, but more than a slave, as a dear brother. He is especially so to me, and even more so to you now, both humanly speaking and in the Lord. Therefore if you regard me as a partner, accept him as you would me. Now if he has defrauded you of anything or owes you anything, charge what he owes to me. I, Paul, have written this letter with my own hand: I will repay it. I could also mention that you owe me your very self. Yes, brother, let me have some benefit from you in the Lord. Refresh my heart in Christ. Since I was confident that you would obey, I wrote to you because I knew that you would do even more than what I am asking you to do. At the same time also, prepare a place for me to stay, for I hope that through your prayers I will be given back to you.

CONCLUDING GREETINGS

Epaphras, my fellow prisoner in Christ Jesus, greets you. Mark, Aristarchus, Demas, and Luke, my colaborers, greet you too. May the grace of the Lord Jesus Christ be with your spirit.

DEATH
TO LIFE